SUGAR AND SNOW

Also by Irene Davis

Marie and the Mouse King
Sugar and Snow
Hawk and Hound
Curse and Crown

Reign of the Roses
Secrets of Water and Willow
(forthcoming 2024)

Standalone
Whiskey in the Jar

The Whitford Crew
Anyone But the Earl
Head Over Wheels
The Words and the Bess

SKOOKUM CREEK

SEATTLE

SUGAR AND SNOW

IRENE DAVIS

MARIE AND THE MOUSE KING   BOOK ONE

Editing by Sarah Pesce
Book cover and interior design by Bonnie Loshbaugh

ISBN 978-1-941633-20-5 (paperback)
ISBN 978-1-941633-06-9 (ebook)

Second paperback edition March 2024 by Skookum Creek Publishing

Visit the author's website at www.irenedavisbooks.com

For my grandfather,
who gave me the gift of stories in music.

One

I᷈ᴛ's dusk on the twenty-fourth of December, and I'm sitting alone in the back parlor. The dark creeps up from the corners, along with the chill of winter. I tuck my feet up and curl my toes inside my satin slippers so they don't grow numb.

The doors across from my seat on the sofa are closed, but lamplight leaks around the edges. If I half-close my eyes, it is a frame of light around a portal of pitch black: the entrance to another world, not merely the drawing room.

Every year, my parents throw a party on Christmas Eve, as regular as clockwork. Every year, I wait, imagining that this will be the night when my nutcracker returns. And every year, I have been disappointed.

I twist my fingers in the golden chain around my neck, then untwist them again. I'm eighteen now—much too old for childish thoughts of magic—and yet, still I sit here in the cool darkness, waiting. Suppose this is the year when he returns?

The drawing room doors burst open with a rattle. Lamplight overflows into the parlor. My cat, Maunzi, who has been sitting on the other end of the sofa, leaps down and runs off into a still-shadowed corner as my little niece, Clara, bounces in.

"Aunt Marie!" She climbs onto the green velvet sofa beside

me, not worrying about crumpling her new silk frock. "Why are you sitting in the dark?" she asks, then, not waiting for an answer, demands, "Tell me a story."

"What sort of story?" I ask. My head is filled with the delirium of memories from that other Christmas. The drawing room overrun with mice. My brother's toy soldiers marching into battle. The image of the mouse king scattered across shards of glass: dozens of fierce faces lit by dozens of candle flames. The nutcracker doll leading my brother's toy soldiers and the other playthings into battle. The final bloody duel between the nutcracker and mouse king—all these things swirl in my mind, as they always do in these dark days before the new year, when the world is disordered and the veil of reality seems thin and threadbare against the unknown that waits in the cold winter nights. But Clara is only five; I can't tell any of these things without frightening her.

"Any story you like," Clara says earnestly.

I shake my head, trying to bring myself back to the present moment. The mouse king is dead, and the nutcracker, who promised to return for me, has never come.

He will not come. More than ten years have passed. It was only a childish dream, and I'm too old to believe otherwise. "I'll tell you a story later, Schätzchen," I say to Clara. "Let's go into the drawing room. I have a present for you."

She takes my hand, and we go into the other room, where all is light and warmth and laughter. I give her a whole packet of gingerbread dolls, and she lines them up on the table, naming them for her family: "This is Papa, this is Mama, this is you, Aunt Marie, and this is Uncle Fritz." She looks up at me with wide brown eyes. "Where is Uncle Fritz?"

"He's coming later," I promise, though I'm not certain that he is.

Even though my brother is home from the army on a holiday leave, he tends to disappear in the afternoons with his hussar friends. He returns late, sleeps late, then goes off again. If he comes back for the party tonight, he'll probably bring his fellow cavalry troopers with him, the whole lot of them smelling of beer and smoke and horses. Mother will pretend she doesn't notice, Father will look thunderous, and my sister Luise will say something cutting about proper behavior for gentlemen.

Do hussars count as gentlemen? I'm not sure they do, even if they are a part of the Grand Imperial Army. The hussars consider themselves a breed apart: more daring, more dashing, more dangerous than other cavalrymen, let alone common foot soldiers.

Clara takes a handful of walnuts from the bowl on the table and pretends they are gifts the dolls are giving to one another while I sit beside her and look around the room. My father is greeting guests. My mother is overseeing the musicians who are arranging themselves in one corner of the room.

My sister Luise is by the great Christmas tree with her husband, Johann. It's a quiet moment for them, with Clara out from underfoot. Luise leans her head against Johann's shoulder. Neither of them speaks, and I wonder if I would ever want that with someone—to simply stand quietly next to one another.

From the open parlor door, Maunzi slinks past the toy cabinet that stands in one corner, past the musicians, and the tree, and the tall grandfather clock in the other corner, to disappear out the other door. He will go sulk upstairs until the hustle and bustle of the party is over, no doubt.

Under my eye, the great gilded owl atop the clock looks back at me, lifting its wings and whirring as it prepares to strike the hour. My heart skitters briefly in my chest. The sound of this clock once heralded the arrival of the mouse king.

But not tonight. Instead, my best friend Trudy sweeps into the room with her parents and her younger sisters. I leave Clara with the gingerbread dolls and the walnuts on the tablecloth and go to greet the Wendelsterns.

Trudy is scanning the room when I reach her side.

"Fritz isn't here," I say into her ear when I lean in to hug her.

"I wasn't looking for him," Trudy replies quickly. Water droplets glitter in her hair where snowflakes have melted, but I think the red on her cheeks is more than the cold winter air outside. She is neither a soldier nor a horse, and so Fritz hasn't noticed her blushes and sighs and stammers over the last year. Still, I like the idea of Trudy as my sister, so I haven't tried to discourage her.

I draw her away to the table with Clara, who immediately asks again for her story.

"In the Kingdom of Dolls," I tell her, "there is a lake of rose water, as pink and sweet-smelling as you could ever wish. On the water swim silver swans with golden necklaces on their long necks. They don't eat bread crusts like the swans you know, but only marzipan. Would you like to visit the lake shore and feed the swans?"

But Clara shakes her head. She doesn't want to share her sweets with birds, however beautiful they might be, and her attention is wandering. There is so much to see around the room. She slips down from the table and goes with Trudy's younger sisters to investigate the shining treasures in and around the Christmas tree.

I stay with Trudy. The Aschenbrandts have arrived. Petra and Magda join us, and we all exchange stories about the things we saw on our separate visits to the Christmas market until there is a banging and clattering in the entrance hallway.

At first, I can't see through the crush of bodies in the room. Then there is a flash of emerald green, the crowd parts, and Godfather Drosselmeier is there.

He twirls the green cape from his shoulders and reveals a large package in his hands, tied up with a wide red ribbon. Little Clara creeps close to Luise's skirts with wide eyes, and my sister puts a protective hand on her daughter's shoulder.

Godfather Drosselmeier is uncanny, with his wrinkled face, his shining white wig, and the large black eye patch which takes the place of his right eye. If I were to see such a strange-looking person on the street, I know I ought not to stare—and yet, I believe that he enjoys the effect he has on people, that he wants to be stared at. No one, I think, would insist on wearing a violently yellow frock coat all year round if they didn't wish to be noticed.

He stands in the middle of the room, grinning brazenly at the guests and making a spectacle of himself. Another swoop of his cape, and the single package has become three, stacked together in a precarious tower atop his outstretched hand. Clara claps, and the adults murmur appreciatively, even though Godfather plays these tricks with his presents every year.

He hands the smallest parcel to Luise, the middle one to me, and the largest one to Clara, who pulls at the ribbon immediately. The wrapping falls open. There is a doll inside, slender arms upstretched above her dress, which has skirts like pink flower petals.

Clara lifts the doll from the box, but before she can do more than stroke its painted face, Godfather Drosselmeier plucks it from her hands. With a dramatic flourish, he inserts a little golden key into the doll's back through a slit in the fabric of her dress.

There is a clicking sound as he winds its mechanism, then he sets the doll on the table, and everyone watches as it begins to dance.

Luise and I open the other two packages, and there are two more dolls in purple and red costumes. We hand them over for Godfather to wind up, and soon all three are moving across the tabletop. Each doll spins to the left while raising its right arm, pauses, takes a step and blinks its painted eyes, then reverses its arms and spins in the other direction.

By the time the third doll is wound, Clara is already fidgeting. I'm looking for the polite words to thank Godfather for the beautiful dolls that can only be looked at and must therefore inevitably join the ranks of similar puppets on the highest shelf of the toy cabinet. I'm too old to play with dolls, the way I ought to be too old to believe in magic.

Before I can form the right phrase, however, there's a fresh commotion at the doorway. Fritz enters with his fellow hussars. They are dressed as splendidly as his toy soldiers ever were, with dark green attila jackets and the matching pelisses fastened over their left shoulders all smothered in yellow braid. Unlike the toys, however, these cavalrymen are tall and vigorous, and the floor shakes under the stamping of their boots.

The table, too, vibrates with their arrival. The dancing dolls tip over on the tablecloth, arms still twitching. There is a delicate grinding as the mechanisms attempt to spin the prone bodies and fail.

Godfather Drosselmeier scowls and reaches for the dolls. Luise helps to right them, but Clara runs to Fritz. I turn away from my godfather's glowering eye and follow after the child. Trudy, Petra, and Magda follow after me toward the cavalrymen.

Behind us, I can hear my godfather muttering dyspeptically while Mother and Luise soothe his wounded feelings. Fritz has always been the least appreciative of Godfather Drosselmeier's gifts, seeing no purpose to figurines that only move in a set pattern over and over. Our godfather spends so much time on his clockwork mechanisms, and I ought to be more appreciative—but I'm glad for my brother's interruption.

Fritz catches Clara up and tosses her into the air. "Again!" she cries, and he obliges while the rest of us look on.

When he has sent Clara flying half a dozen times and she is breathless with laughter, he sets her down and pulls an orange from the dangling sleeve of his pelisse. "Merry Christmas, Schmusebacke."

The other troopers make a semicircle around us, all inquisitive eyes and pert mustaches. They smell not of beer, but of mulled wine from the Christmas market: warm spices and citrus overlaying the wool and leather scents released by the snow which has melted into their uniforms. One of them elbows Fritz with a mischievous look in his dark eyes. "Are all of these young ladies your nieces, Stahlbaum?"

Fritz rolls his eyes, but he introduces us to his fellow hussars, even the ones who are from our city and already well-known to us. He delights Clara by naming her "Mademoiselle Clara Kaltenborn," as if she were a grown lady. Even if nothing else magical happens this evening, it feels like a small miracle to see these tall young men, softened by the holiday atmosphere, bending low to kiss Clara's hand as if she is a princess.

She manages to keep up a dignified facade until the dark-eyed trooper who asked for introductions kisses her hand. He has a particularly luxuriant mustache, and she giggles when it tickles her. Immediately, she is mortified by her outburst and hides her face in my dress.

"Ah, Mademoiselle Kaltenborn, forgive me," he says and winks at me. "I didn't mean to offend you with my whiskers." When she is coaxed to look at him again, he makes a great show of twisting the ends of his mustache until she smiles shyly at him.

Fritz introduces me and Trudy, and the Aschenbrandt sisters as well. The dark-eyed hussar is called Dietrich Lang. He has the same lines of golden braid on the cuffs of his jacket as my brother, showing his rank as a lieutenant. When he bows over my hand, his mustache doesn't so much tickle as tingle. My skin feels peculiar under his touch: too hot, too cold, too tight, too… *something.*

He straightens, but his hand lingers on mine, and there is something in his eyes I can't define. Expectation, perhaps, but what does he expect from me? I know my skin is turning pink under his gaze, and I'm as flustered as little Clara was. I don't want hussars to wink at me or kiss my hand or smile at me in the way that Lieutenant Lang does.

"What an unusual necklace you wear, Mademoiselle Stahlbaum," he says, and I'm glad for the excuse to pull my hand from his. My fingers find the delicate chain at my throat and the seven circlets strung on it.

"It was a gift from a friend," I say. "I wear it in remembrance."

"It's a lucky man who is remembered by such a lovely lady," he says, his gaze lingering at my collarbone.

"Yes," I say, grabbing Clara and retreating quickly. Only as I walk away do I realize I didn't say the rings were given to me by a man.

Two

Petra and Magda stay to talk with the hussars, but I take Clara back to Luise, trying not to feel the gaze of the cavalrymen on my back. Trudy comes with us, though not without a glance over her shoulder and a breathy little sigh. She and Fritz have one thing in common, I think. They both find the sight of him in his uniform very pleasing.

I look back, too, and meet Lieutenant Lang's eyes again. Immediately, I turn away.

He's no different from the other hussars. Of course, they're not all lieutenants, but meeting his gaze shouldn't affect me any more than looking at my brother. They are both tall, both smiling, both wearing the same uniform—but I don't dare hold Lang's gaze. If I look too long at him, I'm afraid I won't be able to look away.

Clara goes to her mother. "Look," she says, showing off her prize. "Uncle Fritz gave me an orange."

"Do you want help opening it?" Luise asks. She's still at the table beside Godfather Drosselmeier, who is working on the dancing dolls. They lie on the table, stripped of their fine dresses. Their faces are turned to the side, and now the red-painted cheeks look as if they are ashamed of their nakedness.

Next to the dolls, Godfather has spread his clockwork tools out on the tablecloth in a neat line of tiny metal implements I can't name.

It's one thing to see him working on the gears within our tall grandfather clock and quite another to watch him rummaging about inside the open torso of a female form with her bare legs akimbo. It makes me feel ill. I don't want to see this peculiar scene, and suddenly I'm quite sure that I don't want Clara to watch it, either.

"Come and see what's in the toy cabinet," I say to her, but she's staring at the naked dolls.

Godfather Drosselmeier looks up from his macabre work and fixes his single eye upon me.

"Click and whirr, whirr and click,
This pretty little doll
Took an unexpected fall
And now her gears all stick."

As he recites his rhyme, he jabs inside the doll with one of his tools. Luise winces, and I try not to grimace at the horrifying sight.

"I'm sure you'll have her fixed up soon," I say as he finishes his rhyme. Then I grab Clara and Trudy and pull them both to the far side of the room, away from Godfather Drosselmeier and farther away from the hussars. "I'll show you the toys your mama and I played with, Schätzchen. Would you like to see my favorite doll?"

I open the tall glass doors of the cabinet and take down the doll I named Mamsell Trudchen after my best friend. Her porcelain face is smudged with persistent dirt, and her dress shows just how many times she was served with tea and bread and jam by my small, unsteady hands in years past.

Trudy rolls her eyes when I introduce the doll to Clara. "Marie is only trying to flatter me, Clärchen. That is her favorite doll, up there." She points to one of the higher shelves where the nutcracker stands. Despite the years which have passed since that Christmas when he first arrived in our house, his lovely violet uniform is still as smart as any of the cavalrymen Fritz has brought with him tonight.

"He's not a doll, he's a soldier," I say, but I see how Clara's eyes light up when she sees the little man on the shelf. He looks back at her with his kindly face and painted smile.

"He's still a doll," Trudy says.

"Not just a doll," I say, taking him down and setting him in front of Clara. "This nutcracker once saved my life, you know."

Clara looks at the nutcracker, with his large head and torso balanced on spindly wooden legs. Then she looks up at me, as if sensing the story she demanded earlier is imminent. "How, Aunt Marie?"

"One Christmas Eve," I begin, "when I was only a bit bigger than you, Schätzchen, I stayed up very late. I should have gone to bed with everyone else, but I was playing with my new toys and didn't want to put them away just yet."

I pause, looking for the right words to tell the story to her. I'm not the storyteller. Petra is the one always coming up with new and fantastic tales to entertain us at our little sewing circle. I only have the one story, all the more wondrous for being true. No one ever believes it when I tell it, but the memories stay with me, cold and dark and inevitable as the snowy night outside.

"When the clock struck midnight," I continue, "I suddenly heard the sound of little feet all around the room. A great army of mice had come in, ready to eat up all the gingerbread and sugar dolls and apples on the Christmas tree. They came over the floor, right up to the footstool where I was sitting."

Clara clutches Mamsell Trudchen tightly. "What did you do?"

"I climbed up on the stool," I tell her. "I was about to scream for help when there was a commotion in the toy cupboard. The nutcracker jumped down from the shelf and called

Uncle Fritz's toy soldiers to arms. Under his command, they drove the mice away and saved me. The nutcracker himself borrowed a sword from one of Uncle Fritz's cuirassiers and slew the king of the mice with it."

I pick up the nutcracker and straighten a piece of the braid on his jacket. "And all this he did while gravely injured!" I hold out the nutcracker for Clara and Trudy to inspect, pointing out the line beneath his teeth where he's been repaired. "Uncle Fritz made him crack too large a nut and broke his jaw, so he ought to have been in bed recovering, but he still came to save me." Then, because it is Christmas Eve and I know I should act charitably even though Godfather has unsettled me, I add, "Godfather Drosselmeier was his surgeon after, and you can see he's practically as good as new."

Clara sets Mamsell Trudchen down and looks the nutcracker over carefully. I watch her discover the wooden cape at his back that acts as the lever to open and close his mouth and remember how delighted I was with the toy when I first saw him.

If it was not a dream, if he really were to return for me, I know that he would be a perfect gentleman, for all that he wears a hussar's uniform.

"Can we feed him a nut?" Clara asks, admiring his sharp white teeth.

"Yes, let's put the little man to work," says another voice.

I startle and nearly catch my fingers in the gold chain at my neck, where they have strayed unconsciously. When I turn, it is Lieutenant Lang who stands there with one shoulder propped on the corner of the toy cabinet. How did I not notice him approach? I was too deep into my memories and dreams, losing track of the real world again.

He waves to the table, where the bowl of nuts is set out among the other holiday treats. "Shall I fetch some nuts, mademoiselles?"

"Yes, please," Clara says. She looks up at him, then turns to me and holds up the nutcracker. "Please, Aunt Marie?"

But I shake my head, trying to calm my heartbeat and find my voice. I take a breath and say, "Thank you, Lieutenant. But I don't want to reinjure him, poor fellow."

Lieutenant Lang pushes off of the cabinet. The glass panes of the doors rattle, and I cringe inwardly, thinking of one of the details I left out of the story for Clara: how, during the battle, I stumbled against those cabinet doors with disastrous results. It's not overly visible in the golden light of lamps and candles in the drawing room, but my left arm still shows a spiderwebbing of white. I can't help putting my hand over my elbow to cover the scars.

"Very well," the lieutenant says. His mischievous grin has returned, and there are fine laugh lines at the edges of his eyes.

He is dangerously handsome with that smile. I am caught again in the trap of indecision: wanting to stare at him, knowing I should look away.

"Perhaps I'll eat some of the gingerbread dolls if I can't make use of the nutcracker," he says.

"No!" Clara cries indignantly. "Don't eat my gingerbread dolls!"

"Don't tease the child," Trudy says. "Not on Christmas Eve."

"Who says it is Mademoiselle Kaltenborn I mean to tease?" Lieutenant Lang says. He's still looking at me, and I still haven't managed to look away. "Will you really not give up your nutcracker, Mademoiselle Stahlbaum?"

"No," I say. I can feel myself blushing again. Where are the other hussars? If one of them must come to pester us, it should be Fritz so that Trudy can moon over him. Perhaps he's aware of her interest after all and is therefore avoiding us.

"You love this doll so much?" Lieutenant Lang asks. "He's an ugly little thing, really." He looks at the nutcracker's over-sized head and white beard of cotton wool and raises a sardonic eyebrow.

"Yes," I say in frustration. Of course, the wooden doll's features don't compare to the man who stands before me, but that isn't the point. "I do love the nutcracker. Not for his looks, perhaps, but for his noble actions."

Lieutenant Lang tilts his head to one side, his dark eyes flashing. "And yet, you won't allow him to do what he's been made for."

I can't possibly explain what I mean to the lieutenant. He would never believe me; no one has ever believed me. All I can do is glare at him. "We have other nutcrackers," I say. "Of less sentimental value. Let me show you."

I leave Clara and Trudy beside the toy cabinet and stride across the room to the table where Godfather Drosselmeier is still fussing over the dolls. He looks up as I approach, but I'm too focused on dealing with Lieutenant Lang to wait for whatever Godfather might say to me.

There is a perfectly ordinary and serviceable nutcracker beside the bowl of nuts on the table. I pick it up and turn to thrust it into the lieutenant's hand, but at that moment the musicians begin to play. Before I know what he's doing, Lieutenant Lang has passed the nutcracker from one hand to the other and set it back on the table, all while keeping hold of me.

"Would you do me the honor of this dance?" he asks, then tugs me out into the middle of the room before I can reply.

I don't want to dance with him, but I can hardly pull away. I'm too old to pretend I'd rather be with the dolls at the toy cabinet, and I'm certainly not going back to sit with Godfather Drosselmeier and his black looks.

Lieutenant Lang seems to be greatly entertained by teasing me. If I make a fuss about dancing with him, then he'll only be more amused. Besides, if I leave him in the middle of the dance, everyone will see and want to know what has happened. And then what will I say? "This man has been laughing at me with his

eyes all evening, and I find him infuriating" won't win me anyone's sympathies. My only remaining option is to stare angrily at
the lines of yellow braid across his chest.

"You are upset with me, Mademoiselle Stahlbaum," he says,
as if reading my thoughts.

"Nonsense," I say, lifting my chin to look him in the eye.
"It's Christmas Eve. How could I be angry with anyone on a
night such as this?"

"How indeed," he says wryly, and twirls me about.

Unfortunately, he's a masterful dancer, and there's no chance
for me to step on his toes. He leads us through the other cou-
ples easily, past Luise and Johann, around the Ritters and the
Wendelsterns. Fritz is on the sidelines, but Trudy and Petra and
Magda have all found dance partners among the hussars.

At first, I'm angry with Lieutenant Lang for his insult to the
nutcracker, then I'm angry at myself for being so irritated when
he can't know what the nutcracker means to me. He's a handsome officer who is obviously a friend of my brother, who made
Clara smile, and who is neither stepping on my toes nor letting
his hand wander from the proper position at my waist. If he
hadn't said anything about the nutcracker, wouldn't I be flattered
by his attention? I'm being childish when I should be acting like
a proper young lady.

I begin to relax. What does it matter if Lieutenant Lang has
irritated me? It's only one dance, and then I'll have plenty of
other partners. For once, my brother has brought me a pleasant Christmas present, though I doubt he meant it. Tonight, I
will dance every dance with a different young man, all of them
smartly dressed in their fine uniforms.

"What are you thinking of now, Mademoiselle Stahlbaum?"
Lieutenant Lang asks. "Dare I hope it is my company which puts
such a pleased look on your face?"

"You may hope anything you like," I say, because even if
I'm no longer angry, I'm not willing to admit that he's even

partially correct.

"Ah, mademoiselle," he says softly, and a shiver runs over my skin despite the warmth of the room. "You cannot even begin to imagine what I hope for."

I stare up at him and nearly miss my step before he pulls me along.

The music ends. Lieutenant Lang bows, and I curtsy. Another of the hussars is immediately at my side, asking for the next dance. I turn to him with the widest smile I can manage, but Lieutenant Lang turns me over without hesitation.

I dance with each of the other cavalrymen, even a blushing young ensign who can barely meet my eyes. As the evening continues, however, I find my attention straying from my partners to seek out Lieutenant Lang again and again. Is he still watching me? Will he catch me watching him?

He dances with Trudy and Petra, makes a gallant partner for a few of the matrons who are feeling sprightly, then retreats to the edge of the room, talking with Fritz and the other troopers. He doesn't seem to be looking at me, and I try not to feel disappointed. What does it matter if he's paying attention to me or not?

By the time the musicians are growing red in the face and my father calls for a halt to the dancing, I've half-convinced myself that I should apologize to him for my rudeness. Perhaps, after dinner, I will go up to him and try again.

THREE

W<small>E</small> all go into the dining room. Before I reach my seat, however, Luise takes my arm and pulls me aside.

"Well?" she asks.

I look at her in confusion. "Well, what?"

"You danced with half a dozen young men," my sister says. "Was there a spark with any of them?" She looks at the foot of the table where Fritz and the hussars, having come late, are seated in a masculine group.

I follow her gaze and feel my cheeks warming. "I—I don't know," I say.

"What about Ernst Hatt?" she asks, indicating the trooper sitting beside Fritz with an unsubtle raise of her eyebrow and jut of her chin. "The judge's son."

Ernst has been Fritz's friend forever, but he's obviously taken with Petra Aschenbrandt, and he'll never be my nutcracker. None of them will ever be the prince I've been dreaming of for the last decade. Not Ernst Hatt, and especially not Lieutenant Lang, no matter how well he dances.

"'Hussar's wife' is just another way to say 'widow,'" I say to Luise. It's what Fritz says whenever anyone asks when he's going to find a wife, and right now it seems a fine excuse.

My sister frowns at me. "But Ernst won't be in the army forever," she says. "He'll want to settle down when his service is finished."

I don't care the slightest about Ernst, and even if I did, he's in the army right now. Am I supposed to say that I want to wait for him? I already have the nutcracker to wait for. "I'm hungry," I say.

My sister sighs in exasperation. "You're not a child anymore," she says. "It's time you grew up."

I'm not a child, but I don't want to be a grown woman if it means marrying—or waiting to marry—someone who will settle down in the same city he was born in, take his father's job, and never leave. Where's the magic in that? I tug my arm out of my sister's grasp and take my place at the table between Johann and Godfather Drosselmeier.

Godfather barely glances at me as I sit. He is glaring balefully down the table at the hussars, who are laughing among themselves. They're probably telling stories they wouldn't be able to mention if there were women seated among them. At least he's finished with the repairs for the dolls, which have been set to rights and put up on the mantelpiece, safely out of reach of anyone trying to play with them.

The food is brought out, and we all eat. My father and Herr Wendelstern begin talking across the table about the war and where the armies may end up in the spring. Everyone hopes that the front will stay a safe distance away from our city. Our count has joined the coalition allied to the emperor, who everyone agrees is the greatest military commander the world has ever known.

That's what the men are speaking of: how it is only a matter of time before the enemies of the emperor submit and the war is over. Since Fritz and his friends are all a part of the emperor's Grand Army, though, how could they say anything different?

No one expects me to know anything about armies and

emperors and troop movements, so I am free to eat my supper and, I suppose, consider the prospect of marrying a hussar when the fighting is over. I wish the nutcracker would take me away again to the Kingdom of Dolls, where no one will tell me what to do—but when I look up from the table and see the dancing dolls set on the mantelpiece, I'm not sure if I want that either. I wish there were a third option.

On my left, Godfather Drosselmeier has taken over the conversation with stories about the travels of his youth, which took him from his native city of Nuremberg to all sorts of far-flung places. He's in the middle of a recounting of the Battle of Peterwardein—which even I know was a century ago and he couldn't possibly have participated in—when a late visitor is shown into the room.

The new arrival is brilliantly dressed in a scarlet frock coat trimmed with gold brocade. It's almost enough to put the hussars' uniforms to shame, except for the excessive quantities of braid and lace trimmings they wear. His face is young beneath an old-fashioned white wig, and there is something familiar about him, though I can't say what it is.

He moves around the table, offering greetings to my parents and all the assembled guests, while I try to remember where I have seen him before. Nothing comes to my mind until Godfather Drosselmeier, who has been caught up in his own story, looks up and sees the young man. "Nephew!" he cries, pushing back his chair. "You have arrived, at long last!"

"Yes, Uncle," says the young man in the red coat, and my breath catches in my throat. It's a good thing I have no food in my mouth, or I would be choking on it. If this is Godfather Drosselmeier's nephew, then he must be—he *must* be—

The younger Herr Drosselmeier turns toward me. I should rise from my chair and greet him, but all I can do is look up at him. Is it really him? My nutcracker, come for me after all this time? My heart is in my throat, and my palms are damp with nervous sweat.

He smiles at me and produces a packet of gingerbread dolls, nearly the same as I gave to Clara and which Lieutenant Lang threatened to eat. "For you, Mademoiselle Stahlbaum," he says, holding them out. His smile slips a little. "Though you are much grown from the image I had of my uncle's dear goddaughter. I have been away for too long, perhaps."

His eyes are a peculiar color, greenish but very pale. His mustache is thinner than the whiskers Lieutenant Lang tickled Clara's hand with—but why does Dietrich Lang persist in coming into my thoughts when all of my hopes are finally realized? For it is he, my nutcracker, freed of the curse laid on him by the death of the mouse king's mother, as Godfather Drosselmeier told me of on that extraordinary, sorcerous Christmas.

I look up at him, trying to match the features I know from his painted face to this new form he wears. Too late, I realize that he's still holding out the gingerbread dolls. I haven't taken them, and everyone at the table is watching us curiously. Even the hussars have stopped their talk to stare at me and the nutcracker.

"Thank you, Herr Drosselmeier," I say, and take the packet of gingerbreads from him. Our fingers brush, and I wait for the zing of emotion to run over me—but there is nothing. I cast my gaze downward, confusion welling inside me as I stare at the gingerbreads without seeing them.

Why is he here now, halfway through the Christmas Eve celebration? He was supposed to return as the triumphant prince of the Kingdom of Dolls he once transported me to and carry me back there to be his princess. He doesn't look like a prince now—he looks like a bit of a fop.

When my father rises to direct the rearranging of chairs to seat the younger Drosselmeier at the table, I see that he isn't even particularly tall. He comes only to the level of my father's nose, which means I'll be a finger's width taller when we are both standing.

Immediately, I chastise myself for these mutinous thoughts. It doesn't matter a whit if he's tall or short. As I told Lieutenant Lang when he pronounced the wooden nutcracker figurine ugly, it is not for his looks that I love him, but for his deeds.

I look at young Herr Drosselmeier through my lashes. I love him, and I have waited every Christmas Eve for him to come for me. But the fleeting sense of familiarity I felt on first seeing him has disappeared and, try as I may, I can't get it back. The more glances I steal in his direction, the more of a stranger he seems. When he catches me looking at him, however, the smile he gives me is entirely familiar and knowing.

I turn my head away and find myself caught, instead, in Lieutenant Lang's dark gaze. The cavalrymen on either side of him are speaking to each other while he stares down the table at me and Herr Drosselmeier. *You see*, I want to say to him, *here is how a gentleman acts: bringing gifts to a young lady, instead of teasing and staring and startling her.*

But I'm not going to speak with him. I'm going to leave with my nutcracker and go into the magical realm of the Kingdom of Dolls, and never see Lieutenant Dietrich Lang again. I look instead at the familiar faces around the table: my parents and their friends, Luise and Johann and Clara, Trudy and her family, my brother, Petra and Magda—is this also the last time I will see them? What happens after I go with young Herr Drosselmeier into the Kingdom of Dolls?

The meal is finished. Our cook, Dora, has gone home to her own family already, so I help clear the plates. It gives me a few moments in the kitchen, away from everyone's eyes. My sister has been watching to see if I am looking at any of the hussars, Godfather Drosselmeier has been watching to see if I've been listening to his stories, Herr Drosselmeier has been watching me, my parents, Lieutenant Lang, Trudy—I feel like one of the toys in the glass case, with everyone waiting to see what motions I will go through if my spring is wound.

I pile the plates on the counter and go to the back door. The kitchen is warm from the stove, so I open the door a crack. A winter wind comes in, and I stand for a minute, looking out into the snowy dark and letting it cool my face. What if I were to simply walk out into the back garden? I could cross to the stables, surely full of the horses belonging to the hussars, and ride away into the night to find my fortune. *Fly*, the wind seems to whisper in my ear. *Fly away.*

But I don't fly away. I have no wings. My head might be in the clouds too often, but that doesn't lift my feet from the ground. I close the door and shut out the wind, then turn back into the house and my family.

In the dining room, the company is still talking and making merry. My father has moved his chair to sit next to Herr Ritter, the two of them with their heads together and likely discussing business, for all that it's a holiday. I can see Trudy near her parents, trying to surreptitiously watch the hussars and probably waiting for me to come and gossip about the cavalrymen with her.

The cavalrymen are laughing uproariously amongst themselves. Of course, the moment I look at them, Lieutenant Lang looks up. His gaze meets mine. My breath catches and my skin prickles, as if the cold wind has followed me in from the kitchen door.

Then one of the other cavalrymen says something, and Lieutenant Lang turns back to laugh with his fellow troopers. His eyes release mine, but my heart still beats overfast.

I look for an empty seat, somewhere away from the hussars. The table is still strewn with sweetmeats, sugared almonds and gingerbreads and baked stollen packed with nuts and raisins. Someone has fetched the bowl of nuts from the drawing room, and young Herr Drosselmeier is cracking nuts for the others. He has inherited some of my godfather's sense of showmanship, for he makes a spectacle of it: with his right hand he puts a nut into his mouth, then with his left he tugs at the queue of his wig as he cracks the shells.

Those nearest him are watching with good humor, and Clara, sitting on Luise's lap, looks utterly entranced.

Herr Drosselmeier cracks open a hazelnut, catches my eye, and holds it out.

I shake my head. "No, thank you," I say.

He shrugs and gives it to Clara instead. She takes it, watching him with the fascination I want to feel but don't—and suddenly it's all too much. The food I've eaten curdles in my belly, and I know I can't rejoin the party right now. Instead, I slip away, out of the dining room, through the drawing room, back to the cool, quiet solitude of the back parlor.

I perch on the sofa and press my cold fingers against my overheated cheeks. After more than a decade of waiting, this night is finally to be the continuation of that distant Christmas Eve when the nutcracker first appeared in my life, and my most overwhelming emotion is confusion.

My hand strays to the golden chain at my neck, and I slide the circlets through my fingers, counting them. One, two, three, four, five, six, seven. The seven golden crowns of the mouse king, presented to me by the wooden nutcracker after he had defeated that foe in battle. They are too big for rings, yet even when I was a child they were too small to serve as bracelets. For a while, I kept them in my jewelry box, then I hit upon the solution of wearing them on a chain, as I do now. In this way, I have kept the reminder of the nutcracker and his deeds with me for over a decade.

As the years have passed, I've often imagined how the nutcracker would return for me. It always seemed that he must come on another Christmas Eve and take me again to the Kingdom of Dolls, where we would rule together with occasional visits to the neighboring Kingdom of Chocolate or Paperland.

But now I'm revising my assumptions. Herr Drosselmeier is no longer a doll, so what business would he have in the Kingdom of Dolls? Everything there was made of sugar and sweets: marzipan castles with orangeade fountains, gingerbread houses with roofs of candied lemon peel, lakes of rose water, seas of almond milk. It seemed like a pleasant dream when I was seven; it sounds like a perpetual tummy ache now.

I'm not a child anymore, and the more I think about what my life might be if I go with my nutcracker, the more my doubts grow. If he has come for me, do I still wish to go? He is my hero. He killed the mouse king for me. And yet—

Footsteps in the drawing room distract me from my thoughts. I draw away from the patch of light by the doorway, not wanting anyone to find me. Is it Trudy or Luise, come to search me out and bring me back to the others?

If it is Herr Drosselmeier, will he want to leave now for the Kingdom of Dolls? It's everything I've wished for years, but I'm not ready. I want to stay with my family and friends. I want to tell stories to Clara. I want to see if Fritz will ever notice Trudy.

I think of the poor naked dolls beneath Godfather Drosselmeier's hands and shudder. No, it's not even a question in my mind. I don't want to live in the Kingdom of Dolls.

I draw my feet up on the sofa, folding myself as small as I can, and listen to the footsteps as they circle the other room. There is a rustle and a few musical tinks—whoever is in the drawing room is looking at the decorations on the tree, disturbing the branches and the ornaments of tin and glass. Then the steps approach the back parlor, and a figure blots out the light in the door frame. I wrap my arms around my chest, hugging myself in the darkness—but it isn't Herr Drosselmeier who enters the room.

It is Lieutenant Lang.

FOUR

"MADEMOISELLE Stahlbaum," Lieutenant Lang says. The light from the drawing room glints in his eyes. "Forgive me for intruding upon you."

"Have you lost your way?" I ask, unfolding my arms and sitting up straight. Perhaps I can direct him to the privy and be done with him.

He shakes his head, and the candlelight sparks in his eyes again. "I am exactly where I mean to be," he says.

Before Herr Drosselmeier appeared, I'd decided to be polite to Lieutenant Lang. Perhaps he, too, means to apologize, or perhaps, like me, he wanted a quiet space away from the party. At the very least, he's not going to take me away from my family. By the beginning of the new year, the hussars will return to their garrisons. Whether I go with the nutcracker or not, I won't see the lieutenant again after this evening. I can be a gracious hostess and give the room up to him.

I rise from the sofa at the same time that he steps forward, and suddenly we are standing face to face. I try to change direction, lose my balance against the sofa, and stumble.

Lieutenant Lang catches me by the arms. Suddenly he fills up all of my senses: the heat of his hands on my bare skin, the scents of mulled wine and leather, his face so close to mine as he says, "Don't go just yet."

"Lieutenant," I say. The word comes out far breathier than I intend, almost a gasp.

He lets go and steps back a little, though not far enough that I can easily move around him. "Your necklace," he says. "Will you give it to me?"

My hands fly to my neck, and I clutch at the golden circlets. "No," I say. Then, "Why?"

He looks down, not at my bosom, but at my hands on the necklace. "Because," he says.

I grip the circlets tighter, feeling the edges of the metal press into my skin, and shake my head. For years, this necklace is all I've had of the nutcracker, the proof that I didn't dream that long-ago battle. When I first showed the circlets to my family and told them the story, they only laughed and shook their heads. Godfather Drosselmeier even tried to claim that he himself had given the circlets to me, as charms from his watch chain. But I know the truth: that they were the mouse king's crowns before the nutcracker gave them to me.

And then Lieutenant Lang takes a breath and says, "They are mine."

"No," I say. Now I'm glad that the sofa is right behind me as I collapse onto it, staring up at Lieutenant Lang—the mouse king who cannot be a lieutenant, cannot be a man, cannot be here. "You are dead," I breathe.

"Obviously not," he replies. "Though I have come too close too often." He holds out his hand to me. When I don't move, he sits down on the edge of the sofa and hooks a finger under the golden chain of my necklace.

I freeze as he slides his hand along my skin, collecting the seven crowns within his fingers. He rubs his thumb over them, and the motion sends his knuckles tapping against my collarbone. Each movement reverberates like thunder through me, or perhaps that is my heart beating like a wild thing caught in a cage.

He leans nearer, and a shiver runs over me. We're alone, and he's much too close. This is the sort of situation that young ladies are always warned against. I should scream and push him away, but I can't move.

"They make a pretty ornament for you," he says. "But I will take them back now."

"And then what?" I whisper.

"Never fear, mademoiselle," he says. "My quarrel is not with you, but with my mother's murderer." The words feather over my skin as he reaches around to the nape of my neck and undoes the clasp of the necklace. "Thank you for keeping these safe for me."

"No!" I say. "You can't—" and then there is someone else in the darkened parlor with us, rushing to pull Lieutenant Lang away from me.

"Get away from her, you fiend!"

It is young Drosselmeier—my nutcracker come once again to save me. As Lang stands and looks down at Herr Drosselmeier, however, I'm not sure that I'm the one who needs rescuing. Whatever else Lang is, or has been in the past, the hussar uniform he wears now says he's not to be trifled with, nor will he resolve his quarrels with a few rational words.

"You," Lang says, in the same tone one might use when discovering maggots in a sausage you were about to eat. My nutcracker glares up at him in turn, head high and jaw set beneath his powdered wig. He's not afraid. After all, he has defeated this enemy before. He will do it again, and this time, Lang won't return.

Then Lieutenant Lang looks between me and Herr Drosselmeier and smiles, slow and terrible. My stomach drops, but the nutcracker maintains his heroic pose.

"Oh," Lang drawls. "Yes. I see exactly how it will be." His

smile widens, and his teeth show white in the half-light. "Go ahead, then. Challenge me for the honor of this beautiful young lady."

In the shadowed room, Herr Drosselmeier looks very grim. Nevertheless, he puts his hand to the sword at his hip, a weapon I had thought purely ornamental, and says, "I will have satisfaction from you for the insult to Mademoiselle Stahlbaum."

"Indeed," says Lieutenant Lang. "And I will have satisfaction from you, for all of your sins." He strides to the door leading back to the drawing room. "Come, let us do the thing at once." He glances back over his shoulder to see if Herr Drosselmeier is following, which he is, still with his face all set in hard lines.

He looks almost like the wooden figurine, and I suddenly wonder what happened to it. Is it an empty shell back on the shelf in the cabinet? Did it disappear when Herr Drosselmeier walked in the door?

"Now, then," Lieutenant Lang is saying. "The challenge is yours, which means the choice of weapon is mine."

I hurry into the drawing room after the two men. Lieutenant Lang stops in front of the Christmas tree, bathed in the golden glow of dozens of tiny candles. I look beyond him to the tall grandfather clock, with the owl crouching on top. It is past eleven. Soon it will be Christmas, and yet here are these two men, about to fight a duel, to resume the battle that took place in this same room on that other Christmas. The scars on my elbow seem to prick me and I rub at them.

This isn't how it is supposed to go. This isn't the continuation of the story I wanted.

"Pistols would end things too quickly," Lieutenant Lang says. "I think it must be blades."

"I shall finish you," Herr Drosselmeier replies, "as I should have done before."

Fritz comes in the door on the other side of the room with two of the other hussars. Soon they will have seconds chosen, then they will march out into the snowy night, and then what?

"Stop," I say. "Stop this at once. You can't fight, not on this night when we're meant to remember the meaning of love and family."

Both men turn to look at me, their faces variations on a theme of masculine surprise at an unexpected feminine disruption. "It's Christmas Eve," I remind them. "You can't duel tonight, nor tomorrow." I lay a hand on Lang's arm and lower my voice so the others in the room won't hear. "Give me back my necklace, Lieutenant, and let us all forget this foolishness."

"What's going on?" my brother asks. "Lang and Drosselmeier are to duel?" He looks at them, then at me. I can see the speculation written all over him. The last thing I need added to this situation is for him to put his head together with Luise and her ideas about marrying me off.

I look back at my brother and wonder what to say. *It's nothing, just that your friend is the nightmare monster who used to come to my bedside and scare the wits out of me as a child, and he's stolen my necklace, which might actually be his anyway.*

No, I definitely can't say anything like that. The merest suggestion that Lang has been in my bedchamber will be nothing but trouble, even if it was more than a decade ago, and he wore a vastly different form. "They are not going to duel," I repeat. I step away from Lang, turning instead to Herr Drosselmeier. He has to be more reasonable than Lang. He will listen to me. "You can't duel on Christmas."

Lieutenant Lang laughs, and there is a bitter edge to his humor that I hadn't noticed earlier in the evening. Then he sketches a courtly bow, managing to direct the courtesy exclusively to me even though Herr Drosselmeier stands beside me. "As the young lady wishes," he says. To Herr Drosselmeier, he says, "I will see you at first light on the twenty-seventh. Pray, do not disappoint me."

He turns precisely on the heel of his well-shined boot and

strides out of the drawing room. The guests who have crowded in from the rest of the house part wordlessly before him, turning their heads as they try to stare equally at Lieutenant Lang, Herr Drosselmeier, and me. I want to run after Lang and convince him to change his mind, but I'm hemmed in by the crowd.

Trudy threads through the room and takes me by the arm. "Marie," she asks in an urgent undertone, "what has happened?" My mother appears on my other side, her brow heavy with worry. I let them escort me upstairs, away from the growing buzz of curious voices.

What has happened? So much that I'm struggling to piece it together myself. If Lang is the mouse king, then he didn't die when the nutcracker fought him before. Yet the nutcracker was able to take his crowns and give them to me. And now, they will fight again if I can't think of some way to put it off permanently.

In my room, Trudy seats me on the chair before my dressing table. In the mirror, I see her concerned face, along with my mother's. The lamps are low, but do they see the high color on my cheeks?

"What happened?" This time it is my mother who asks.

I meet her gaze in the glass. She loves me, I know, but she's always been impatient with my "flights of fancy," as she terms them. If I tell her about Lieutenant Lang and Herr Drosselmeier's true motives for fighting, she'll only sigh and wring her hands. Isn't it enough that her quiet Christmas Eve gathering of family and friends has been doubly spoiled by Fritz tromping in with half a legion of cavalrymen and by my provoking a duel among the guests?

"It was too warm in the dining room," I say, "so I went to sit in the back parlor for a few minutes. I didn't light the lamps, so Lieutenant Lang didn't see me when he also came into the room. I was lost in my thoughts and didn't notice him either until he nearly sat upon me. I'm afraid I was so startled I screamed, and Herr Drosselmeier assumed he'd done me some injury." I bend my lips into a smile and give a little shrug. "They can't have a duel on Christmas, and I'm sure we'll be able to sort it out tomorrow when everyone's heads have cooled."

It sounds a weak story to my own ears, but my mother nods and rubs her temples. "Oh, Mariechen," she says wearily. "Luise never got into half the trouble you do."

"Yes, Mother. Luise has always been very practical," I say.

"I must go back downstairs and help to smooth things over," she says, too distracted to chide me for being snippy. "You'd better stay here. It's time everyone went home to their beds, anyway."

"I'll stay with you," Trudy says quickly.

"Yes, of course," my mother says. She sighs and leaves us, muttering under her breath.

"He sat on you?" Trudy asks as soon as we're alone. "Surely he didn't!" She casts a skeptical eye over my pale blue dress, which is unlikely to blend into the green sofa even in the dark.

"No," I admit. "He sat next to me and said some very strange things."

Trudy's eyes widen. "What sort of strange things? He seemed so charming!"

I bite my lip and move around the room to turn up the lamps, banishing the shadows to the corners. I want to tell her the truth, but the words won't quite come out. She believed my stories when we were children, but it has been years since we spoke of my adventure with the nutcracker. "He took my necklace," I say finally. "That was really what made me cry out."

"Your necklace?" Trudy echoes. She comes closer, looks at my bare neck, and makes a soft sound of dismay. "The brute! But why?"

"He said it was his." I touch my skin, feeling the place where the necklace used to lie. The place where Lang's fingers grazed over my skin, gathering up his crowns. "I think he must be mad.

Or I am."

"Oh," Trudy says. She nods, but she doesn't tell me I'm not mad, and her face still looks puzzled. I should say more, but I can't shake the memory of the disbelief on my family's faces when I told my fantastic tales before. I stay silent, but long after Trudy and the other guests have departed the house and I'm in my bed with Maunzi at my feet, I lie awake in the dark hours of the night, wondering.

FIVE

O N Christmas Day, we go to church. In between services, I huddle with Trudy or pester Fritz for information about the duel. He is peevish and irritable, as underslept as I am, but with a hangover on top of it. By the time the Christmas dinner of roast goose is being set out on the table, I've worn him down.

"Fine," he says, half-snarling. "I'll tell you. Only leave a man alone with his aches and pains, Marie."

"If they're fighting over me, I have every right to know," I say for the thirty-seventh time.

He scrunches up his face and rolls his eyes at me. I wish Trudy could see how ugly and rude he looks right now; it would put the idea of marriage right out of her head. No one should marry Fritz when he makes faces like that. I would tell him so if he wasn't about to give me the information I so desperately want.

"I said I'll tell you," he says irritably. "It's to be at the field outside the eastern city gate. The snow is well flattened there, and it's not far from Herr Wendelstern's home if we need to fetch the surgeon."

"Thank you," I say, trying not to think about what the surgeon would be required for. "Thank you, Fritz."

"You must stay out of the way," he warns. "Don't do anything foolish."

"Of course not," I promise, because I don't intend to. But on the appointed morning, as I hurry toward Trudy's home on my way to the eastern gate, I am filled with foolish thoughts.

Maybe Lieutenant Lang is mad. Maybe Fritz told him my tale of the nutcracker, and he's imagined himself into the role of the mouse king—but I can't truly bring myself to doubt his sanity, when so many people have doubted mine. I only want it as an excuse. If he's not in his right mind, then they can't duel. If he's telling the truth, there is no way around it.

When I think of Lang's words, however, I know he is deadly rational. He's exactly where he means to be, with events unfolding exactly the way he wants them to. So, what of the nutcracker?

He fought the mouse king before, but now Lang is a hussar and a soldier in the emperor's army. Whether Herr Drosselmeier has been in the Kingdom of Dolls, or trapped within the wooden nutcracker, or somewhere else entirely, it doesn't seem likely he can have the fighting experience that Lang has.

Trudy comes out of the Wendelsterns' home before I can even try to signal her. She's bundled against the cold. Beneath her wool hood, she squints at the gray sky, where the first hints of dawn show on the horizon. "Let's go," she says. "We don't want to miss it."

I nod and take her mittened hand in mine. We hurry toward the eastern gate.

There is no sound but the creak of the hard-packed snow beneath our feet. Even the little sparrows that peck for crumbs throughout the winter are snugged up somewhere warm this early in the morning. Not until we slip out the gate and are on the far side of the city wall, do we hear the jingle of horse's bridles and the grim tones of male voices carrying through the frigid air.

Two knots of men stand in the middle of the field, while the horses are picketed to one side. Herr Drosselmeier's short form is at the center of one group; the other coalesces around Lieutenant Lang. As Trudy and I near the men, I see my brother standing apart from the group around Drosselmeier, watching but not taking a side. He gives me a sour look, but doesn't shoo us away.

One of the hussars leaves Herr Drosselmeier's side and approaches the men around Lieutenant Lang. Would Lieutenant Lang like to apologize and avoid potential bloodshed? But Lieutenant Lang's sneer is clearly visible, even in the pale, watery light. He sends Drosselmeier's second back with a definite refusal.

Now Lang's envoy should go to Herr Drosselmeier and, in turn, give him a chance to withdraw the challenge. But no one leaves the group around Lieutenant Lang, who is occupied with unfastening his pelisse. He is already bare-headed; one of the other cavalrymen holds his shako with its tall ostrich plume.

Trudy pauses to greet Fritz as I run to Herr Drosselmeier. "Mademoiselle Stahlbaum," he says with genteel surprise. "You should not be here."

"Please," I say. "Don't do this."

"I'm afraid I must," he says. "But fear not, my lady. Once I have defeated him, we will return to my kingdom, as I have promised."

"I don't want to go," I blurt, then clap my hands over my mouth.

The nutcracker blinks at me with his odd green eyes. "But, mademoiselle," he begins.

"I'm not a child," I say. "I don't want to live in a land of dolls and sugarplums. Let us stay here, in the real world, where we can be with my family and with yours."

He shakes his head. "I will defeat my enemy," he says. "Then we will go where he cannot follow, and you shall be a princess beside me." He turns away from me and begins unfastening his overcoat, clearly with every intention to go through with this and no intention of listening to me.

In desperation, I run across to the other group and Lieutenant Lang, with Trudy trailing after me. When I plead with him, he's no more willing to give up the fight than Herr Drosselmeier. In the cold dawn, Lang is hard-eyed. There's no trace of the laughing mischief he showed during the Christmas Eve party.

He jerks his chin toward the city gate. "Go home, mademoiselle, unless you wish to see your cavalier's life blood spill in the snow."

Trudy gives a little gasp beside me. "Will you not fight to the first touch?" she asks.

Lieutenant Lang shakes his head. He has removed his pelisse and jacket. Next, he pulls a silver chain from around his neck, tucks it into the jacket, and begins to undo the laces of his shirt. "I will kill him," he says calmly.

"Why will you not listen to reason?" I ask. "You are mad!"

His hands still, then he reaches out suddenly and catches me by my chin. Trudy makes another little squeak, but I can't look away from Lieutenant Lang.

"I am angry," he says. "But not mad." Each word falls slow and deliberate, like rocks into a deep pool. "You know what he has done to me, mademoiselle, and you know my reason."

Lang lets go of me, and I take a step back, my heart hammering wildly. His hands return to the laces. I see the flash of gold on his fingers. The circlets I wore around my neck are now distributed among his fingers, each of them a perfectly fitting ring. Then he reaches up and behind his shoulders, grabs a handful of linen, and hauls his shirt over his head, revealing his torso.

There is a massive scar across his chest, white and puckered. At first, all I can do is stare. How long did it take him to heal and recover from that terrible slash? It must be the near-fatal blow he received from the nutcracker at their last meeting.

When I remember myself and look away from his bare chest, Lieutenant Lang is giving me a bitter look. "He killed my mother," he says. "I couldn't save her, but now I have a second chance to avenge her. I will not spare him for your sake. Go home, mademoiselle. I will not say it again."

"No," I say. "I beg of you, do not do this!" But Lieutenant Lang turns away, no longer listening to me.

He is the mouse king. He is the monster from my childhood, and he is taking the korbschläger he carries from its scabbard.

I spring at him, beating at his bare back with my mittened hands and crying out every curse I know.

The other hussars push me back. Fritz and Trudy—my friend suddenly turned traitor—take me by the arms and pull me away to the edge of the field.

"Let me go, Fritz," I sob. "Let me go! Can't you see? He's the mouse king. He will kill the nutcracker!"

My brother takes me by the shoulders and shakes me. "Marie!" he says. "Stop it. You are hysterical."

"Don't you remember the story Godfather told us?" I ask desperately. "The fairy tale about the hard nut. The queen of the mice put a curse on the princess, and when young Drosselmeier had broken it, she tricked him into stepping on her and breaking her back. Then he was cursed and became the nutcracker."

Fritz shakes his head. "It was only a story, Marie," he says. "Godfather told us many such."

"He means to kill him," I say. "He took back his crowns from me, and now he will kill Herr Drosselmeier and complete his revenge."

"You are speaking nonsense," my brother says.

"I am speaking truth," I say desperately. "What do you know of Lang? Does he speak of his family? It is no accident that he came with you to our Christmas party."

Fritz looks at me, still frowning.

"Look at his scar," I insist. "Remember that Christmas when Godfather brought the nutcracker? When mice ate all the ginger-bread dolls and gnawed at the marzipan and the sugar figurines, so they had to be thrown away? Until you gave me a saber from one of your cuirassiers for the nutcracker. He defeated the mouse king, but he must not have killed him, and now somehow he's come back as Lieutenant Lang."

"Mariechen," Trudy says gently. "This all sounds quite fan-tastical."

"I retired one of my toy cuirassiers," Fritz says slowly. "I remember that. I wouldn't have given you the saber, except that I'd told one of the colonels that he was honorably discharged and would have no need of his weapon."

There is a clash of metal behind me. I twist out of Fritz's grasp, but it is too late. While we've been talking, while I've been struggling to convince my brother to believe me—the contest has already begun.

The two bare-chested men circle in the snow, each apprais-ing the other. Lang is a head taller; he'll have the advantage of reach as well as everything else.

Still, Drosselmeier steps up to strike at his opponent. Lang parries with another clang, then they both spring back and circle again. They repeat this a few times, each engagement lasting a few beats longer. Their breath makes little puffs of white, visible against the dark trees on the far side of the field. The other men stand back, making a wide ring around them but leaving a larger gap around Fritz, Trudy, and me.

Then Lang does something odd with his feet and lunges at Drosselmeier with unexpected speed. Drosselmeier dodges, but too slowly. The unbuttoned point of Lang's rapier pierces deep into his left shoulder.

Someone screams, and afterward I'm not sure who it was:

Trudy, or me, or Drosselmeier. Perhaps it was all of us at once. Lang has already pulled his blade from Drosselmeier's flesh and retreated. I bite the inside of my lip, watching the grimace of pain on the nutcracker's face.

"First blood," calls a man from Drosselmeier's side. "Enough, gentlemen."

But neither man concedes. Again they circle, blades poised and ready. I can see the dark trickle of blood on Drosselmeier's white shoulder. I imagine it is steaming in the cold air. Around them, the other men shift their feet and exchange glances. Should they try to stop this? Can they?

I feel the same tension in my brother, who still holds my arm. I glance at him and see that Trudy, who has let go of me, is clinging to his other side. Her father is a surgeon, so I know she's not afraid of blood, but she's not above taking the opportunity to move closer to Fritz, either.

On the field, Drosselmeier can no longer hold his left arm properly. The wound Lang has given him must be deep, for the arm hangs uselessly at the nutcracker's side, and blood trails all the way down to the waist of his breeches. Why does he not concede? He must be in terrible pain.

Lang moves in on him again. Drosselmeier parries, but Lang's high strike wasn't a true attempt. He twists around and slashes low. This time he opens a long, shallow gash over Drosselmeier's ribs before he retreats. Drosselmeier's futile reply is too late; Lang is already out of his reach.

Drosselmeier is bloodied twice over and hasn't yet put a single mark upon Lang. I feared that he would be unprepared, but I didn't expect he would be this woefully inadequate. If I thought this was really about my honor and not about the old revenge Lang seeks, I would be ashamed of my champion's showing. Instead, I am only afraid for him.

In Godfather's story, his nephew, as a youth who hadn't yet shaved or worn boots, was the only one who could break the legendary krakatook nut and cure the cursed princess. The princess was freed, but rather than marrying her, young Drosselmeier accidentally broke the back of the mouse queen and was changed into a nutcracker himself. He must've wished he'd stayed home in Nuremberg, rather than listening to his uncle's promises. He's probably wishing it now.

The nutcracker is sickly pale, and his movements are slow and clumsy. When Lang lunges in at him with a dizzying barrage of strikes and thrusts, he can barely keep up his defense, let alone find a place to strike back at his tormentor. He takes a third cut, this one a red crescent across his left cheek.

It's not right. Lang is bigger and stronger. He has masterminded this whole situation to his own advantage. I don't know when or how he transformed himself from a mouse into a man, but this isn't a fair fight.

I take off my mittens and stuff one into the other to give it some heft. Then I throw it with all my might at the two men. It hits Lang, glances off his side, and falls uselessly on the churned snow.

Lang looks toward me. It's only for a moment, but it's a distraction, and I think *Now!*

Now Drosselmeier should press the advantage and attack. He should end this terrible duel, and we will call Trudy's father to patch them both up, then all go on with our lives.

But Drosselmeier doesn't attack. He drops his sword and runs to me.

No, not to me—past me, towards the city gate.

I stare after him. Everyone stares.

Even Lang, who has up to this point anticipated his adversary's every move, is momentarily stunned by this outright cowardice. Then he sprints after Drosselmeier.

SIX

HERR Drosselmeier runs headlong to the eastern gate. He slips in the snow, recovers, and continues his flight. Lang gives chase, his long korbschläger still in his hand. As he barrels past our little group, however, Trudy sticks out her booted foot and trips him.

Lang goes down hard, diving forward and almost turning the fall into a somersault. The soft snow throws him off-kilter, however. He ends flat on his back, staring up at the white winter sky.

Lang lies prone for a moment, his broad chest heaving. The wind is knocked out of him, I think. Trudy's done him more hurt with one movement of her foot than Drosselmeier did in several frantic minutes with his korbschläger.

Then he stands in one powerful, fluid movement. His ragged scar is even more prominent now that his skin is reddened with physical exercise. His sword is still in his hand, but the impact of his tumble has bent the slender blade nearly double. He tosses it away, turns his face to the sky again, and lets out the most terrifying roar of frustrated anger I have ever heard.

Everyone stands frozen on the snowy field as the echo of Lang's cry fades away. Then he turns to our little trio and stalks forward. Trudy shrinks against Fritz, who puts an arm around her. Whether he cares for her or not, he's a soldier first.

"You!" Lang growls at me as he advances. "Again you thwart me!"

I'm sorely tempted to cower against my brother as Trudy is doing, but the other cavalrymen are closing around us. They came here on this frigid morning to witness a duel of honor, not a murder. If Lang attempts to throttle me with his bare hands or something similarly vicious, my brother and the other men will stop him.

There is no doubt in my mind now that Lang is mad, but it is a different madness than I first suspected. How can he not be mad? Between the actions of Godfather Drosselmeier and his nephew, Lang's entire family is dead. My siblings can be over-bearing and infuriating, but I can't imagine my life without them or my parents. Lang's madness is a grief that cannot be born, and yet he has borne it—carried it with him until it has festered into the terrible septic anger I see in his eyes. So instead of cowering away from him, I step toward him.

He glares at me and bares his teeth, as he did when I was a little girl and he was a nightmare crouched on my bedside table, threatening to chew my beloved nutcracker to bits. But I'm no longer a seven-year-old hiding beneath the bedclothes, and he's no longer a mouse. He is a man, capable of rational thought. If I can only convince him to listen to reason, there must be an end to this conflict.

"If you kill him," I say, "it won't bring back your mother or your brothers. You are poisoning yourself with your quest for revenge. You must give it up. Please, I beg you."

Lang stares at me for a moment longer, then his face cracks open into something that would be a smile, if the expression were not so tortured. He laughs. It's a bitter, hollow sound that echoes in the open space between the city wall and the forest.

"Ah, Mademoiselle Stahlbaum," he says, and I hear a faint

ghost of the wry humor he showed during the Christmas Eve party. "I forget that you are so young, and your life has been so simple. Do you think I don't understand the nature of mortality? I know my family is gone. I know I am the last of my line. But that only makes it easier to dedicate myself to my singular purpose."

He steps away, and I see his bare chest rise as he inhales a deep draught of the cold morning air.

Then he shouts to the city walls, to the forest, to the sky, to all of creation: "Drosselmeier! You cannot escape from me! I will find you!"

I look to the city gate, but the nutcracker is gone. Does he hear Lang's declaration? Even if he doesn't, he must know the truth of it already. Despite my warm coat, I shiver.

"Did I do right in tripping him?" Trudy asks me as Lang walks away from us.

"Yes," I say. I would have done the same had I thought of it. I'm glad the nutcracker escaped, even if I don't exactly understand why he ran away.

Across the expanse of trampled snow, Lang is putting his shirt and other layers of clothing back on. The remaining hussars are collected in little clumps, talking among themselves and shaking their heads. Someone picks up the two korbschlägers: the intact one Drosselmeier dropped, and the crumpled one Lang tossed away. Drosselmeier's scarlet frock coat they leave lying in the snow.

Trudy wraps her arms around herself and chafes her shoulders. Fritz let go of her and stepped away the moment Lang was no longer threatening us. Trudy looks sidelong at my brother, but he's staring at the city gate where Drosselmeier fled.

"I thought he was a soldier," Fritz says. He shakes his head and adds, "Only the coward retreats."

"What will happen to him?" I ask.

"Perhaps he'll die of shame," Fritz says uncharitably. "Certainly he can never show his face amongst fighting men again."

"Lieutenant Lang forced him into the fight," I say.

My brother waves his hand dismissively. "That doesn't signify. He should have met his foe with bravery and honor."

"Even though Lieutenant Lang was trying to kill him?" Trudy asks. "It doesn't seem honorable to me."

Fritz draws his brows together in a frown. I expect him to say something rude, perhaps tell us that women can't understand these affairs of men, but he only shakes his head again. "Let's go," he says. "It's over. You've seen all that you wished to, haven't you, Marie?"

He leads us toward the city gate. Drosselmeier is nowhere to be seen, though a few spatters of red in the snow show where he passed. I look back to the field, where Lang is buckling his fur-lined pelisse over his jacket. If the cold managed to touch him, its effects will soon retreat. He is whole and untouched, while Drosselmeier ran away half-dressed and bleeding. If he doesn't get indoors quickly, the weather will finish what Lang began.

Young Drosselmeier may have shown himself a coward, but his other option was death. Would I rather that he was a rapidly cooling corpse here in the snow? A brave death is still a death. He may not have acted as a gentleman should, but I don't think he deserves to die.

If anyone is to blame for this, it's my godfather. It was his mousetraps that killed the mouse queen's first seven sons. It was his decision to bring his nephew to break the curse, and it was he who brought the nutcracker doll to me on that long-ago Christmas Eve.

I look back as my brother pulls me toward the gate. Lang vaults up onto his horse, a bay with a bald face. The white marking covers so much of its head that it looks almost skeletal. It sidesteps restlessly as Lang settles into the saddle.

Lang wraps his hand in the reins and wheels the horse

around. The stallion tosses his head, then rears, slashing the air with his hooves. A war horse, ready to accompany his master into battle. Lang is steady in his seat as the horse returns to the earth, and I see his face is still set with anger.

For a moment, I wonder if he will spur his horse over the city walls. I imagine the snow flying under the animal's hooves, the way its hindquarters would coil for the soaring leap over the heads of open-mouthed city guards on the wall. And then, Lang and his stallion thundering through the narrow streets, hunting the younger Drosselmeier down like a terrier after a rat.

Or perhaps Lang will ride straight to Godfather Drosselmeier's workshop. Those sharp hooves, trained to split skulls, will crash through the door and scatter clockworks in all directions. Then what? What defenses does my godfather have?

No mousetrap could contain Dietrich Lang as he is now.

But Lang doesn't ride into the city. He turns away from the eastern gate and rides away into the forest. As he enters the trees, the morning sun makes its appearance in the narrow opening between the horizon and the flat gray clouds above.

Long spears of light cut through the bare trunks and ignite the frost-coated branches with a pearly golden glow. A wind whips suddenly across the field, reminding me of the words I thought I heard on the wind when I looked outside the kitchen door on Christmas Eve. What would the wind have to say about this morning's events? Perhaps it whispers to Lang, too.

I don't hear any words this time, but the wind kicks up ice crystals that glitter in the sudden light. I blink against the brightness and when my vision clears, Lang is gone.

Fritz tugs at me again. "Come on, Marie," he says. "You'd better be home before Father and Mother start to worry, or I'll never hear the end of it."

I look down and see my bare hands. "My mittens!" I run to fetch them where they lie on the snow. Granules of ice cling to the dark blue wool and sting my skin when I brush them off.

The whisper of the wind is still in my thoughts, and I have a sudden irrational desire to run into the forest after Lang. I could ask what he intends now toward the two Drosselmeiers, uncle and nephew. I could try again to stay his hand.

When I hesitate in the middle of the field, though, my brother calls my name.

He's at the absolute limit of his patience with me; I can hear it in the tone of his voice. If I don't come immediately, he will catch me up, sling me over his shoulder like an unruly parcel, and carry me home to the disappointment and censure of the rest of the family.

So I don't run into the forest. I go with Fritz and Trudy, back into the city. The townspeople are awake now. Smoke streams from the chimneys as fires are stoked and breakfasts prepared. Voices carry through the streets as neighbors call to one another, offering holiday greetings and anticipating the new year.

We stop at the Wendelsterns'. Trudy goes in, and Fritz waits at the door with me until she comes back to report that her father is still abed. Young Drosselmeier has not come to the surgeon for his wounds.

Fritz sucks his teeth and makes a sound of disappointment. "Only the coward retreats," he says again. The words have a well-trod sound to them, as if it is a motto he has learned and repeated often. Something carved over the door of his barracks as a daily reminder to every trooper in his regiment, perhaps. Words that might be emblazoned on the hilt of his saber, or embroidered on the bandeau of his shako hat. *Only the coward retreats.*

Is my nutcracker a coward? No. I refuse to think it is cowardice to protect your own life.

And what of Lang, then? He can't leave the death of his family unavenged, for that doesn't seem right either, but must the repayment for death be more death? He is a hussar, now, and must think the way they do: honor and bravery above all. Lang cannot retreat from the battle he has entered into, for only the coward retreats.

What good are honor and bravery, though, if you end up honorably and bravely dead? I look at my brother, but his face says he's in no mood for such questions. I keep my thoughts to myself and hurry to keep up with him.

We pass the Ritters' cook after we leave the Wendelsterns' home. I see the glint in her eyes as she recognizes us, then I realize that others are staring at Fritz and me as we walk down the street. Gossip about the duel between Lang and Drosselmeier has spread from the guests at our family gathering, and people lean away to whisper behind their hands as we pass.

They probably don't know yet how the duel ended—that's a story that will keep everyone talking until spring at the very least. I keep my head up and face straight ahead. What's one more story about me, that Stahlbaum girl who lets her imagination run away with her? At least this time, no one can deny what has happened. Trudy and Fritz were there, and half a dozen other hussars, all witnesses to the duel. It happened; it wasn't in my head.

Fritz hears the whispers as well. By the time we reach our own home, he's scowling worse than ever. "Go upstairs," he says as we enter the front hall. "I'll talk to Father."

I don't want to go upstairs. I want to stay and see what happens next. It's the same impulse that would have sent me into the forest after Lieutenant Lang, even though I know him to be the monster of my worst childhood nightmares. "No," I say to Fritz.

He glares at me. "You're in enough trouble as it is," he says. "And I'm your elder brother. You should obey me."

"I won't," I say.

Fritz narrows his eyes and clenches his jaw, and I lift my chin. Before we can settle into the argument, however, the front door behind us bursts open, and Luise's husband, Johann, nearly knocks us both over.

"Is she here?" he demands. "Clara—is she here?"

"Why would she be here?" I ask.

"She's gone," he says. His eyes are wild, his chin is dark with stubble beneath his mustache, and his overcoat is buttoned crookedly.

"We only just returned home," Fritz says. "I don't know if she's here."

My mother is likely still dressing, but the noise draws my father into the foyer. Johann repeats his question, but my father shakes his head.

I thought the worst had already happened this morning when I was unable to stop the duel between Herr Drosselmeier and Lieutenant Lang. Then I thought the worst moment was seeing my nutcracker—my protector, my champion, my cavalier—turn and flee. That moment was immediately overturned when I witnessed Lang's shout to the sky, but even that was nothing beside the sick mixture of nausea and fear and dread I feel now as we search our house and then make a second search of Johann and Luise's home, as we send word to friends and neighbors and call out Fritz's friends to quest through the streets on horseback, and still there is no sign of my niece.

SEVEN

THE rest of the day is spent in the parlor of Luise and Johann's small house. The room is crowded with whispers and glances as Luise and my mother talk with an endless round of visitors. Some come with genuine concern, but others are here merely for the gossip.

I sit in the corner and make a pretense of sewing. Trudy and Petra sit with me for a while, Trudy with her own sewing and Petra with her quill and little sheaf of papers. Trudy and I sew, and Petra writes out a clean copy of one of the sewing circle stories. She sends them away to a scholar friend of her father's, who means to publish a collection of stories one day.

The hours slide by. Petra finishes her writing, rubs her ink-stained fingers, and says she must go home again. Trudy, too, has to leave to look after her younger sisters. They each kiss my cheek and tell me that Clara will be found soon. After they're gone, I go back to my sewing and stare at it, hoping they are correct.

All the while, we've been waiting for the men to bring us some word from the search. Each time the front door opens, Luise starts up from her chair, and my mother makes a sign against evil. I keep putting my hand to my collarbone, expecting to find the seven gold circlets beneath my touch, then remembering belatedly that they aren't there.

The clock on the mantelpiece chimes, and Luise looks at it apprehensively. Our elderly neighbor, Theda Doerffer, pats her hand. "Don't worry, dear," she says. "Your child is in God's hands."

"They will find her," my mother says. "I'm sure of it."

I'm not sure of it. I still have the awful feeling in the pit of my stomach, and though Luise's cook set food out for us, I haven't been able to eat more than a few bites. There is too much that has been strange and supernatural these last few days. I reach for my necklace again, remember its absence, and turn the motion into a wave to catch my mother and sister's attention instead. "I want to go out and help with the search," I say.

They look at me with identical expressions of surprise and anguish.

"Absolutely not," my mother says. "One missing child is enough. I couldn't bear it if anything were to happen to you, Schätzchen."

How can she still think I am a child? I have had a duel fought on behalf of my honor. It wasn't the whole reason for the duel, of course, but no one said, "Oh, no, you can't fight over Marie—she's just a child."

Clara, though—Clärchen is still a child, even younger than I was when I first met the nutcracker and the mouse king. Where does a five-year-old girl child disappear to on a bitterly cold morning in the dead of winter?

I pick up the embroidery I'm supposedly working on: a pillow slip that will be part of my trousseau. The rabbit I've added looks peculiar. I should probably take the time to carefully pull out the threads that make up its ears and try again, but I can't make myself do it. What use are embroidered rabbit ears when Clara is out there somewhere, cold and alone?

This time, I catch my hand before I lift it. I don't have my necklace anymore. Dietrich Lang has it. I saw the circlets on his fingers.

What did he do with the gold chain? I can allow that the circlets are his, but the chain was mine. I should have followed him into the forest and demanded it back, except that he was on horseback and I was on foot and I never would've caught him. Now, he's gone, and Drosselmeier's gone, and so is Clara. I hope that my niece's disappearance is unconnected to these two otherworldly men, and yet I can't stop thinking about my conversation with the nutcracker this morning. I told him I didn't want to go to the Kingdom of Dolls. What if he took Clara instead?

The front door slams. Luise jumps, and my mother moves to soothe her. I set aside my sewing and go out of the parlor without asking permission. In the front hall, I find Fritz and Johann. The heavy gray promise of the morning's clouds has been fulfilled, and they are both dusted in white, with flakes of snow quickly melting from their mustaches. They look grim and tired and cold.

"What news?" I ask, but Fritz only shakes his head.

The men take off their coats, and Johann walks heavily to the parlor. I tug on Fritz's arm so that he stays back. "What about Drosselmeier and Lieutenant Lang?" I ask. "Is anyone looking for them?"

"Lang can take care of himself," Fritz says impatiently. "And I don't care what happened to young Drosselmeier, even if he is Godfather's nephew. He should have acquitted himself better."

"That's just what I'm afraid of," I say. "What if he's done something else awful? What if he has something to do with Clara disappearing?"

Fritz has been fidgeting and pulling toward the parlor, but these words stop him. Lang rode into the forest, but Drosselmeier went into the city. Who's to say where he fled? This house isn't so far from the eastern gate.

I hope that I'm wrong. I've never wanted more to be wrong

about something in my whole life. Perhaps Clara is playing a silly child's prank—she might yet be found inside a linen chest, sleepy and confused. But we've opened all the linen chests, and the dread that has been with me since the morning still gnaws at my insides.

"I can't stop thinking of it," I say. "If no one knows where Clara is, and no one has seen Herr Drosselmeier either…"

"We'll look for him," my brother says grimly.

In the parlor, Fritz eats the food Luise and Mother and I have been ignoring, then he and I slip out. Mother nods distractedly as we go; I expect she thinks Fritz will take me home. Instead, we go to Godfather Drosselmeier's rooms.

When I was a girl, his workshop was a magical, mysterious place. The tables and shelves are lined with treasures: brightly painted birds carved from sweet-smelling wood, green glass bottles full of apothecary's powders, scraps of silk in rainbow colors, brass cogs and wheels smaller than my fingernail or larger than my whole hand.

In one cabinet, Godfather keeps a clockwork ship that can sail across a tabletop on hidden wheels. It rocks gently as it moves, as if buffeted by the waves of an invisible sea, and two carved wooden crewmen move to adjust its sails while a sea bird flaps its wings at the top of the mast. A prototype, Godfather Drosselmeier told us, for one made of gold and ebony for the amusement of a king and his guests at table during banquets.

"Godfather Drosselmeier," Fritz calls as he hammers on the door with his fist. "Are you at home?"

No answer comes. We exchange a look and Fritz pushes at the door. It's not locked, so we go inside. The workshop is dark, but we open the shutters to let in the fading afternoon light. Godfather's tools are neatly arranged around his workbench, and his stained gray work apron hangs on its hook. The brass ship is in its glass-fronted cabinet, but the workshop has a still and desolate feeling to it. The air is chill. When I look into the stove,

I see only a few small coals glowing in a sea of dust-gray ash.

In the back room, we find a pile of bloodied linens on the bed. The wardrobe stands open, and when I look inside, I'm seized by a memory: the nutcracker stretching out his hand and telling me earnestly that this is not the easiest way into his kingdom, but it is the quickest.

"What are you staring at, Marie?" Fritz asks.

"When I went with the nutcracker before," I say, "it was through our wardrobe, the one that stands by the front door. I was doll-sized with him, and he pulled down a set of stairs from Father's overcoat. We climbed up through the sleeve and came to the Kingdom of Dolls."

My brother takes off his hat and tucks it under his arm, careful not to damage the proud plume that stands up from the front. Then he runs his free hand through his crumpled hair and shakes his head. "Marie," he says wearily.

"But you *saw* them," I say. He has to believe me this time. He must. "You saw Drosselmeier cracking nuts at the Christmas table. You saw Lang's scar. You saw how angry he was."

"Some men lose their minds in battle," Fritz says. "I haven't seen it in Lang before, but I haven't seen him take an interest in a woman, either." He looks at me, narrowing his eyes. "What passed between him and you, Marie?"

"Nothing," I say quickly. "He was only waiting for Drosselmeier to appear." I start to reach for the necklace, then rub my face instead. I'm tired, and this is bringing us no closer to finding Clara. I go back to the wardrobe and stare at the overcoat hanging there while Fritz huffs disapprovingly behind me. Then I look lower, and my heart hiccups painfully in my breast. On the bottom of the wardrobe is a pair of tiny child's slippers.

"Fritz," I whisper. "Look."

He looks where I'm pointing, and then he balls his hand into a fist and smashes it against the side of the wardrobe. The contents—two yellow frock coats, one white shirt, and a heavy overcoat with a fur-lined collar—sway inside. "But where are they?" he asks.

"In the Kingdom of Dolls," I say, staring at the swaying overcoat. If I knew a way to pull stairs from a coat sleeve, I would do it. Then I could follow after the nutcracker and get Clara back.

"There is no such place," Fritz says shortly. He turns and stomps out of the inner room. I follow him. Before I can find a new way to try to convince him, the door opens, and Lang arrives with a gust of winter wind. He looks every bit as angry as he did this morning, but he stops short when he sees us.

Fritz steps in front of me. I don't think he's really conscious of doing so, but Lang looks ready to commit further acts of violence. Actually, he's probably about to accuse us of hiding the two Drosselmeiers, or thwarting him in his quest for vengeance again. I move away from the inner door and tug Fritz with me. "He's not here," I say. "Neither of them. You can search for yourself, if you like."

Lang crosses the workshop in a few long-legged strides and enters the second room. Inside, he turns in a slow circle, taking in every detail of the space where Godfather Drosselmeier eats and sleeps. Despite leaving behind his bent korbschläger this morning, he has acquired another sword, the cavalryman's more usual saber. He pulls it free of its sheath and uses the blade to pull back the bedding.

There is nothing beneath the coverlet, and he growls in frustration. I'm growing quite familiar with the sound. Next, he turns to the wardrobe and raises his saber, as if to slash at the contents. I jump forward. "Wait!"

Lang turns his glittering gaze on me. "Mademoiselle Stahlbaum," he says crisply. "I do not have the patience for social niceties right now."

To meet his eyes, I have to sidestep away from my brother, who is still acting the guard dog. Now it is Fritz tugging at my arm, but I have to speak to Lang. If we hope to follow Godfather Drosselmeier and his nephew to find Clara, then he can't cut the overcoat to ribbons.

"I know where they've gone," I say.

Lang closes the distance between us almost before I finish speaking. His naked blade is still in his hand, and again my brother moves protectively in front of me.

Fritz's hand goes to the hilt of his own blade. "Lang," he says, with a warning in his voice.

Lang glances at him, then sheaths his saber with a snick and says, "Where?"

"The Kingdom of Dolls," I say. "He took me there once." Quickly, I explain about the journey through the sleeve of the overcoat.

Lang listens with narrowed eyes. I can't look away from him as I speak. I need him to believe me. I try to judge his mind from the angle of his dark eyebrows, from the thinning of his lips, from the way his shoulders shift beneath his pelisse. He must believe me. He must help me get Clara back.

But as I speak and his face remains a mask of anger gone cold and congealed, my words falter. No one has ever believed me about my encounters with the nutcracker. So many times I have told the tale and been dismissed for my excessive imagination—even by Godfather Drosselmeier, who was a witness to the opening scenes of my fantastical experience and should have confirmed my words.

I fall silent. Lang nods once and returns to the wardrobe. This time he takes the cuff of the overcoat sleeve in two fingers, inspecting it. "The Kingdom of Dolls," he says softly, contemplatively—almost as if he believes me. He is himself a creature of uncanny magics, after all. Perhaps my story is entirely pedestrian to him, and he will simply nod and follow after the nutcracker.

"You must take me with you!" I blurt out as he tugs at the

sleeve.

"No, Marie," says Fritz. "I forbid it."

Lang drops the coat sleeve and turns back to me. "This is no pleasure jaunt, as you took when you were a child, Mademoiselle Stahlbaum," he says.

"He's taken Clara," I say.

"The child?" Lang asks.

His mask slips momentarily. There is a flash of concern on his face, and suddenly I want to cry. Clärchen—Schätzchen! I will hold her on my lap and tell her stories for a week straight if we can only get her back.

"She went missing this morning," says Fritz. "We've been searching all day."

I close my eyes and press my hands against my eyelids, trying to hold in the tears. My brother puts his arm around my shoulders, and I lean into him, but only for a moment. I don't want Lang to think I am weak. I must be strong enough to accompany him into the Kingdom of Dolls and fetch Clara back. So I straighten up and open my eyes and say again, "You must take me with you. I've been there before. I can act as your guide."

"Marie," my brother says. "You're not going anywhere. And even if you were, I would go with you, not Lieutenant Lang."

Lang looks at us and shakes his head. "I'm not taking anyone anywhere," he says. "I don't even know if I can reach this realm myself."

I don't believe him for an instant. He will move heaven and earth if they stand between him and his revenge. If the nutcracker has fled to the Kingdom of Dolls, then Lang will find a way to get there.

"You must have some magic in you," I say.

"Some," he admits. "But I do not know this magic." He lifts the coat sleeve again, then lets it fall.

"Then we must find a different route," I say. "There must be other ways."

I look hopefully at Lang, but he doesn't make any suggestions. Instead, his brows come together in frustration. I turn to Fritz, but he only shrugs. He hasn't accused Lang of being soft in the head yet, but he hasn't admitted there is magic in the world, either. Of course, he has no idea how to travel to other realms. It is up to me, then, to find a way to the Kingdom of Dolls.

EIGHT

I GO back out into the workshop and look at the shelves and cabinets. Godfather Drosselmeier's creations surround us, staring with silent, unmoving eyes. They aren't the sugar dolls I remember from the nutcracker's realm, but they are dolls nonetheless. I sit down at the stool next to the worktable and try to think. There must be an answer here that will take us to the Kingdom of Dolls.

Fritz stations himself near me while Lang prowls around the room. His tight movements still hold the coiled promise of vengeance, as if he might reach out at any moment and sweep the contents of the shelf before him to the floor or simply smash everything within reach.

I recoil from the thought. Godfather has done many peculiar things, and frightened me more often than not, but much of what he creates in his workshop is beautiful. "Don't touch anything," I say.

Lang gives me a look of such disdain that I would step backward if I weren't already sitting. But I think of how he didn't question my story about journeying to the Kingdom of Dolls, and I try to look pleasant as I say, "These clockworks are precious." I point to the clockwork ship. "That is the model of one he made for a king."

Lang walks to the cabinet where it sits and stares down at the little brass hull. Then he opens the glass door and takes the ship out. "I know this ship," he says, turning it in his hands. "I have seen the other on my uncle's table."

"Your uncle?" I echo Lang's words back to him as if I, too, am an empty-headed clockwork with no thoughts of my own. How can he have an uncle if all his family is dead? And how can his uncle have had a clockwork my godfather constructed for a king?

Lang sets the brass ship on the worktable in front of me and Fritz. "Yes," he says, as he pulls off his gloves. "My uncle."

I look at Fritz, but he gives a small shrug. He knows nothing about Lang's uncle. He had no answer this morning when I asked if he knew anything of his supposed fellow soldier's family.

Lang turns the mechanism's crank with deft fingers. For the space of a minute, the slow *click-click-click* of the spring winding is the only sound in the chill air.

Fritz and I wait, watching until Lang lifts his hand from the crank and moves the lever that starts the mechanism. Is it the ship, or himself he has been preparing for action?

"I listened to your godfather's story," Lang says as the ship trundles obediently over the surface of the table. I wonder momentarily how he could have heard the story, but, of course, he was a mouse and could have been hidden anywhere: within the walls, under the floors, or simply in some dark corner behind the furniture in my room.

"He told you the tale of the hard nut," Lang continues. "How his nephew cracked it and saved the princess from the curse my mother laid upon her." He picks up the ship and rests his finger against one of the wheels hidden underneath. It turns slowly beneath his touch. On the tip of the mast, the carved wooden bird lifts its wings as if in protest.

"Did you not wonder," Lang asks, "how a mouse came by such powers as my mother had? Did you not wonder why the king was so incensed at the loss of a little bacon?" The ship clicks sharply, and he sets it down. "Did you not wonder why the queen was so foolish as to share with a mouse in the first place?"

I want to ask my own questions, but I can't pull my attention away from the little brass ship, not even to see if my brother is rolling his eyes at the suggestion of magic.

"Let us set those questions aside and ask something more practical," Lang says. "What does a childless king fear above all else?" He raises an eyebrow and tips his head to the side, inviting us to guess.

And I know the answer. Lang has already told us, just as Godfather revealed it in his story so many years ago. "His family," I say.

Lang nods to me, as a schoolmaster might do to a student who has correctly shown the sums on his slate. "Indeed," he says. "Year after year, my mother bore sons." He lifts his hands, so the golden circlets on his fingers catch the fading light. "My uncle had seven nephews before his wife showed the signs of bearing her first child."

One by one, he slides the circlets from his fingers and collects them in his palm. The light is fading, and we haven't lit the lamps in the workshop—and still the crowns shine and glitter. I want to touch them. I curl my fingers into my palms and tuck my hands against my belly so I don't try to snatch them away from him. They were mine for so long, and I itch to feel them between my fingers again.

Fritz says, "Are you telling us that you are a prince, Lang?"

Lang shakes his head and gives his short, bitter laugh. "My mother was a king's daughter," he says. "But the queen was not her mother. Still, she had a place in the royal court, and she married well enough for what she was. My father could never have been king, though perhaps he had hopes for his sons. My uncle certainly thought he did.

"When my uncle's wife finally became pregnant, the court astrologer was tasked with casting the horoscope of the unborn child. He foresaw a daughter who would be cursed and unwed. The king heard his own fears in the prediction, and he ordered the arrest of my mother and her family. My father was executed, but the king couldn't kill his sister and nephews. They were of royal blood, after all, if somewhat diluted. Instead, he locked them away and charged the astrologer with finding a way to remove them.

"The astrologer searched his books until he found a spell of transformation. The deed was done in the darkest hour of night, and afterward there was no human trace left of the king's sister and nephews."

Lang pauses. I have been watching the seven circlets, which he's been rolling from one palm to the other, but I look up and find his gaze on me. He slips the circlets back onto his fingers.

"When my mother realized that she, too, was carrying a child, she lay in her nest and wept. She had lived her whole life in the sumptuous rooms of the castle, and now she was relegated to a pile of rags hidden between the walls while her brother still lived and ate and drank as he'd always done. She had committed no crime except that of fertility.

"Of course, she wished to regain her human form and have her revenge upon the king. But what could she do, beyond muttering threats into her brother's ear while he slept? Her seven sons crept to her side and tried to comfort her, saying, 'We will find a way to break the spell, Mother. We will make our uncle sorry for what he's done.'

"They went to the astrologer's rooms in the dead of night and searched for the notes he'd made before casting his wicked spell, but he'd burnt them. Still, they learned many arcane things, and they told them all to my mother.

"My mother went to the astrologer and begged him to

reverse the spell. He refused her, saying, 'It is written in the stars that you shall suffer a cruel fate, madam, and, once written, such a thing cannot be changed.'

"Faced with this heartless response, my mother grew angry. It was the royal astrologer upon whom she laid her first curse. 'By your foolish meddling with stars and spells,' she said, 'you have cast me out of my home for no purpose. May you also be cast out, and wander in far places to no purpose.' Then she bit his finger and scurried away into the wall while he howled.

"If you remember your godfather's story, her curse was fulfilled, for the astrologer was the clockmaker Drosselmeier's companion for fifteen years of fruitless travel around the world when the krakatook nut they sought was no further away than Nuremberg.

"You know all the rest: how my brothers died in Drosselmeier's mousetraps, and I inherited their crowns, the curse my mother laid on the infant princess, and how she died under young Drosselmeier's foot." He pauses for a long moment, perhaps reliving that instant when he was suddenly alone in the world. "And everything that followed," he adds finally.

I shake my head. "I don't know the rest. What became of you after your battle with the nutcracker? He told me you were dead."

"I nearly was," Lang says. His hand strays briefly to his chest, where I know the jagged scar lies beneath his clothing. How did he survive that wound? I wonder if there is a stain of pooled blood somewhere in our house, hidden beneath the carpets in the drawing room. "I crawled away into the wall and lay there. I did not move, even when I heard the prowling footsteps of a cat."

"Ah, the baker's cat," says Fritz. "I remember that beast. The baker called him the 'Undersecretary for Foreign Affairs,' and you could tell the cat took the appointment to heart." He stops, perhaps seeing the pained look on Lang's face, and adds, "Yes, well, of course the Undersecretary never caught any mice in our house."

"No," Lang says dryly. "I have Mademoiselle Stahlbaum to thank for my survival," he adds. "After the nutcracker took my brothers' crowns and left me for dead, I lived on your stuffed marzipan until I could recover my strength."

He nods to me and smiles his bitter, wry smile. It shouldn't make my breath catch to see that smile turned on me, yet it does. I look down at the table, where the brass ship has stopped, and try to remember Lang as a terrifying mouse, but already the image is fading. He is too real and present before me in his current form: a dark-eyed man in a hussar's uniform. If what he's just told us is true—and it is no more fantastic than any of the other strange events I have experienced myself—then the mouse king was the illusion, and Dietrich Lang is the reality.

"And then what?" asks Fritz. "You bought a horse and an officer's commission? As a mouse?" He shakes his head. "You are a lieutenant for the Empire, Lang. We are rational men. You can't really believe you're a part of my sister's fairy tales."

"Fritz—" I begin.

At the same moment, Lang says, "It is no fairy tale. I saw my mother die before my eyes." He turns away from the table and begins pacing the workshop again.

"Fritz," I say to my brother. How can he disbelieve both of us?

"Why are we standing around telling fairy stories when Clara is still missing?" he asks. "I don't care if Lang says he was born on the moon and wants to fly you away on a magic carpet. It's not going to help us find her."

"It will if he can help me get back to the nutcracker's kingdom," I say.

"Marie!" my brother says sharply. "Enough of this foolishness!"

I want to scream, because it is not foolishness, and he

refuses to see it. But he stands and walks away. Lang has stopped by a window, tapping his fingers against the frost-painted glass, and my brother goes into the back room. I hear him kick the wardrobe and swear.

Everyone is angry and at cross-purposes, and none of us are getting anywhere nearer to what we want. I wish I could have the satisfaction of kicking something too, but I don't have the thick-soled boots of a cavalryman, and I'd probably just stub my toes. Instead, I build up the fire and light the lamps, then I go to stand beside Lang at the window.

"I believe you," I say. "And I'm sorry for what happened to your family."

He turns to look at me. "Why should you be sorry? You aren't responsible for any of it."

I want to say that doesn't mean I can't feel sympathy for him, but I'm afraid he will take it for pity. Instead, I say, "Help me find a way to the nutcracker's kingdom. Help me bring Clara back."

He stares at me with a slight crinkle between his brows, as if he is seeing me for the first time.

"Tell me what you know of his kingdom," he says finally. "Tell me everything."

So I do. I tell him every detail I can think of, and he listens with an intensity that is both unsettling and strangely comforting. He doesn't question a single thing I say, only nods from time to time.

He is *listening* to me. No one has ever listened to my story before, not really. Part of me marvels at it even as I'm wracking my brain for the description of the rose water lake we crossed on the way to the capital of the Kingdom of Dolls, or what damage the nutcracker told me the giant Leckermaul had done to his castle.

Lang doesn't take his eyes from me while I speak. Finally he nods once, decisively.

"Do you know how to get there?" I ask.

"No," he says. "But you have been there once. You will be able to return if you want it enough."

I have wanted to return to the Kingdom of Dolls nearly every day for the last ten years, and never made the journey. I start to say so when I realize that for all of that time I never tried to return. I was waiting for the nutcracker to come and lead me there, as he did the first time.

What Lang is saying is that I can make the journey on my own.

I go back to the worktable and sit down in a daze. I don't need Lang as a guide. I don't need young Drosselmeier, either. I can do it for myself.

NINE

FRITZ comes out from the back room, holding the little slippers in one hand. "We should go home," he says.

"No," I say. "Not until we have Clara." I point to the slippers. "If you take those to Luise, it will break her. And Mother—what do you think it will do to her?"

"Nothing good," he admits. He frowns at me, then sighs. "But we are no closer to finding her than before."

"You know she was here," Lang points out. "That is something."

Fritz nods, but the frustration doesn't leave his face. The more I think about it, the more certain I am that Clara has gone with the nutcracker into the Kingdom of Dolls. For my brother, though, she has simply vanished, like a snowflake on your fingertip.

I've always considered Luise to be the most practical of us, but Fritz is not impractical the way I am. No matter what I or Lang might say to him, he won't believe in magic until it becomes something he can swing a saber at or chase down on horseback. We need some softer, subtler solution now to get to the nutcracker's realm and find Clara, but Fritz is unlikely to see it.

"Let's look in the larder," I say. "Perhaps we'll think better with some food in our bellies."

I don't think I've eaten anything all day. I doubt I'll find any appetite, but my mother has always reminded me that little sleep and little food make for much discord.

I find bread and cheese and some apples that have seen better days and divide them into three portions on the worktable. Though the poor meal is a mockery of the royal banquets the brass ship was designed to accompany, I leave the clockwork in the center of the table.

We eat in silence for a time, then Lang, who has seated himself on the other side of the table from me and Fritz, leans forward. He puts one finger on the brass ship and strokes it contemplatively along the line from bow to stern. I watch the slow, deliberate touch and bite the inside of my cheek, caught suddenly in the memory of his fingers at my collarbone as he gathered up the circlets that now glitter on his fingers.

Then I'm ashamed of myself for thinking of such things instead of how to get Clara back. I fix my gaze on the little ship and turn my thoughts away from Dietrich Lang and onto the problem before me.

The Kingdom of Dolls. Dolls and giants, castles and clockworks and lakes of rose water. If a staircase can descend from a coat sleeve, then why shouldn't this clockwork ship sail from the worktable to the nutcracker's realm? I reach for the ship, and Lang withdraws his hand.

"What are you doing?" my brother asks as I pick up the clockwork.

"Surely it's obvious," I say, even though I know it won't be to him. "I'm going to sail this ship to the Kingdom of Dolls and bring Clara back."

I find the tiny crank at the bottom and twist it, then set the ship down on the table. Now it must sail from this scarred wooden surface to the rose water lake, and I must be on board.

What will happen then? How will I journey through the nut-cracker's realm?

Before the ship can go anywhere, however, Lang puts his hand in its path. "You must take me with you," he says, echoing the words I said to him earlier.

"She's not going anywhere," Fritz says. "And not with you."

"I will look after her, Stahlbaum," Lang says. He places the hand that is not blocking the clockwork ship over his heart. "Your sister will be under my protection, and no harm will come to her. This I swear."

This declaration does nothing to smooth my brother's face, and I'm not sure it reassures me either. Lang doesn't want to go to the Kingdom of Dolls to help me find Clara. He wants to find the nutcracker and finish what they started with this morning's duel. But the idea of traveling alone through the magical world unsettles me. What if I find the giant Leckermaul before I find Clara? What if the nutcracker won't give Clara up to me?

I can't take Fritz with me. He still hasn't acknowledged that such a thing exists. How will the magic work for him if he won't believe in it? Not to mention what he will do when we are there, faced with magical things at every turn. Having a companion like Lang with me could be very useful. He would not stop to gape at the improbability of it all as Fritz might. He would simply act.

Still, my brother's caution holds me back. Perhaps there is more to his objection than the fact that he doesn't believe in the Kingdom of Dolls. Fritz knows something of Dietrich Lang the hussar, when I know little of the mouse king beyond his own stories and those Godfather told us long ago.

Lang wants his revenge. I want Clärchen. Both of us need to find the nutcracker, but what will happen after that?

"Will you help me bring Clara home?" I ask. "Will she also be under your protection when we find her?"

The two men have been staring at one another, each trying to force his own shape of things on the other by the power of a clenched jaw and narrowed eyes. Now they look at me, and Lang breaks out his bitter smile. "Mademoiselle Stahlbaum," he says, "do you not trust me?"

"I don't trust you to think beyond your own revenge," I say plainly. "I won't help you if you won't help me. Will you swear it?"

"Marie," Fritz says, his voice low and urgent, but I can't look at him. Now I'm the one staring down Lang, trying to convince him that my will is the stronger.

But Lang nods, still smiling. For a moment, he looks almost as he did when he came to the Christmas Eve party and maneuvered me into dancing with him. I should be wary now, as I was not then. Am I falling into some new trap of his? He's had years to plan his moves, while I'm a novice in this game where the mouse has become the cat. What power can I hold over him?

"Swear it," I say. "Swear that you'll help me find Clara and bring her safely home. On your mother's memory."

The smile falls from his face, as if it were a clay Fastnacht mask he has been holding up in front of his true expression. I imagine the wry smile shattering to pieces on the workshop floor.

Lang gives me a look as serious as the point of his sword. "If I swear," he says, "then you must also make an oath to me that you will help me find Herr Drosselmeier, who killed my mother, and not stand in my way when I confront him next. Will you so bind yourself, Marie Stahlbaum?"

I hesitate, but only for a moment. "Yes," I say, and repeat the words of his oath. How else will I ever find Clara? And if Lang is with me along the journey, then perhaps I will find some other way to convince him to soften his final blow against the nutcracker.

"Then I will help you find your niece Clara and bring her safely home," Lang says. "I swear it on my mother's memory."

"You are both mad," my brother mutters, but he doesn't

sound entirely certain. Maybe he sees Lang's face, which is too serious to disbelieve. When I look at him, however, Fritz is staring at Clara's slippers, which he set at the edge of the worktable.

Is it winter there, in the Kingdom of Dolls? Is she stumbling through drifts of sugar and snow in her stockings or in bare feet? I think of the pink rose water lake, skimmed over with ice crystals, of the strange creatures living in the nutcracker's realm. She shouldn't be there alone.

But I am coming. I will find her, and if the nutcracker has done her any harm, then Lang will add it to the tally of his sins and make him pay for it.

I shiver, though I'm still wearing my coat. I want there to be an end to this that doesn't involve more bloodshed. Even if the nutcracker did cause the death of Lang's mother, even if Godfather Drosselmeier killed his brothers—but I can't think about death right now. I need to think about Clara. No more delays.

I tuck Clara's slippers and the bread I haven't been able to eat into my coat pockets, then reach forward with both hands. I set one on the clockwork ship and hold the other out to Lang.

It isn't the first direct contact of our bodies, but it is the first moment when I reach out to him, rather than him reaching for me. His hand is warm, and as soon as he curves his fingers around mine, I feel more confident. In my mind's eye, I can see the fluid, predatory grace with which he moved across the snowy field. No wonder he danced so well: he is entirely in control of every movement of his body. Now I'm under the protection of this strange, dangerous, magical man. If I can get us to the nutcracker's realm, he will help me bring Clara home.

The Kingdom of Dolls. The rose water lake in winter. Perhaps it is snowing there, as it did here today, soft flakes falling down to the surface of the water, or swirling sideways in a winter wind.

"What are you doing?" Fritz asks, but I ignore him.

Lamplight glitters on the brass hull of the little ship and

on Lang's ringed fingers—but there will be no lamplight on the lake, just the flat light of winter reflecting from clouds above and water below.

The workshop wavers around us, and Lang draws a sharp breath, squeezing my fingers. I think I catch a hint of roses in the air.

Then Fritz grabs my arm and pulls my hand from Lang's. "Stop it," he says. "Whatever you're doing. Stop it."

The windows rattle with a sudden gust of wind outside and the lamps gutter. The scent of rose water fades, and we are still in Godfather's workshop.

"Fritz!" I cry in frustration. I tug free from his grip and glare at him. "You must let me do this."

"It's not going to work," my brother says, but it will. I was so close. I felt it. Lang was right: I can do this if I want it badly enough, and right now, I want it very, very badly. I want to return to the Kingdom of Dolls. I want to find Clara. I want to show my brother that magic exists and I haven't been telling tales.

I reach for Lang's hand again and grip him tightly. I can feel rough calluses on his fingers and the hard edges of the seven rings, but I focus my thoughts on the rose water lake. I close my eyes to hold the image in my mind. The sweet scent of roses fills my nose and light beats bright against my closed eyelids.

"Marie!" Fritz cries. "Lang—the devil take you—stop!" His voice is fading away, however, replaced by a cacophony of clicking and whirring.

My hand, which was holding the clockwork ship, is suddenly empty. I overbalance and stumble into Lang, who is still holding fast to my other hand. He catches me against his chest. The table between us is gone. The stool I was sitting on is gone.

We are no longer in the workshop.

TEN

Lang holds me folded to him, far closer than when we danced on Christmas Eve. The gold braid on his jacket scratches my cheek, but I can also feel the soft fur lining of his pelisse against my ear. He smells of the cold, clean air of the forest, even through the scent of roses filling the air.

"Do you have your balance?" he asks. I feel the rumble of his voice in his chest and I'd like to contemplate the sensation, but I have to lift my head to answer him.

As I do so, I nearly lose my footing all over again. My legs feel weak, as if I have run a long distance up steep stairs to get here. The ground sways beneath me, and I press my hands against his chest to keep my balance. Lang holds my shoulders until I am steady.

"We did it," I say, slowly turning my head in wonder. "We're here."

We are on the deck of the clockwork ship, and all around us is an expanse of pinkish water. It is winter, just as I imagined. The air is bitingly cold, and the distant shore is shrouded in a mist of falling snow beneath deep gray clouds.

"I did nothing," Lang says. "You did this." He lets go of me and steps away while I am still taking in his words. The wind rushes through the space between us as Lang looks out at the lake.

I have brought us into the Kingdom of Dolls. I take a moment to revel in the sense of accomplishment I feel. I brought myself back to this other realm, and not just myself, but Lang and the clockwork ship as well. No wonder my legs feel wobbly.

"Are we going the right direction?" Lang asks. He gestures widely, taking in the waterscape with his hand as I blink at him, open-mouthed. "You are meant to be the guide in this place," he says pointedly.

Even though we are both surrounded by this magical place, it still feels strange to have someone else believe in the existence of the Kingdom of Dolls, and to ask me questions about it. With Dietrich Lang, however, I must upend all of my usual expectations. I close my mouth and turn a slow circle on the deck, hoping to spot something familiar to head toward.

To our left is a wooded shore, to the right some smudgy hills dusted with snow, or perhaps powdered sugar. Clouds smearing downward from the sky obscure much of the view, and I cannot glimpse the towers of the nutcracker's castle anywhere on the shores of the lake. From the low light, it must be nearing twilight here too.

The wind seems to turn with me, pushing the sails first one direction, then another. The clockwork sailors move across the deck. They must be trying to adjust the snapping sails, but their movements are clumsy, and they cannot grip the ropes. The wooden figures are blocky and unfinished, their fingers undifferentiated and unable to grasp anything. I stare at the blank space where they ought to have eyes. How do they even know where to grab for the lines?

"Are we headed toward the capital, or not?" Lang asks.

I turn from watching the wooden sailors and look out at the lake again.

Last time I crossed this lake, I was in a boat pulled by silver swans. I was taken up with the beauty of the elegant birds, with the compliments the nutcracker paid me, with the wonder of the lake's peculiar water, and all the other magical details of this realm. I didn't take note of any landmarks, and now I can't see anything that seems familiar.

Panic closes my throat and tightens around my chest. If I can't find the proper direction across the lake, I won't be able to find Clara, either. We must at least find our way to shore before nightfall.

Where are the swans? I see no sign of them. They must be huddled up together somewhere away from the winter wind that whistles around us and pushes waves past our ship.

The perfume of the rose water grows cloying, and the cold wind cuts through my coat. My mittens are back in Godfather Drosselmeier's workshop, along with my brother. Fritz must be furious with me. I tuck my hands beneath my arms to warm them.

And then, finally, I see something ahead of us. A distant collection of white specks against the dark shore. The swans—it must be the swans. The huge, magical birds that were one of my favorites when I came here before. Ever since, I have watched the ordinary swans at home and wondered if they ever flew from the everyday ponds near my city to this fantastical lake, or if they tell tales of the silver swans the way we girls tell stories of princesses and giants for Petra to write down during our sewing circle.

I point to the flock of swans. They are the only thing I recognize, the only visible landmark to tie this present together with my past in this place. "We need to go that way," I say. "Towards the swans."

Lang nods and walks to the bow of the ship. He mutters something beneath his breath as he dodges out of the path of the sailor-figures. They are still moving back and forth, grabbing at the ropes but not quite catching them. Maybe he doesn't want to watch their unnatural movements. They didn't seem so jerky when the ship was moving across the worktable, but now that they are as large as I am, every strangeness about their looks and motions is magnified.

I move back towards the ship's cabin—or where a cabin would be if there was a door, which there isn't. There is a bench, however, so I sit down and huddle in my coat. I've spent so much of the day sitting and waiting, but it's a relief now to rest. My whole body feels weary to the bone.

The wind settles behind us, sending wisps of my hair into my face, even though I'm partially sheltered by the low cabin. Lang grips the rail at the ship's prow, facing the far shore like an unusually martial figurehead. The deep green of his uniform stands out sharply against the soft pinks and grays around us. The tall ostrich plume on his shako bends beneath the wind.

The sails are flapping, dragging their ropes back and forth beyond the ineffectual reach of the sailor-figures. Even though the wind doesn't fill them, the ship is moving slowly forward. Perhaps it is the clockwork within that drives us through the water, or perhaps it is some magic of Lang's.

I stare at his back as I rub my hands together and tuck my fingers into my collar to warm them against my neck. He spoke of arcane things learned from the royal astrologer's books, of curses and transformations, but I have no idea what he's really capable of. I haven't seen him do anything magical. There was nothing supernatural in his actions at the Christmas party or in his duel with Herr Drosselmeier. Still, that doesn't mean he can't change the world around us in ways I can't begin to imagine.

A spasmodic movement catches my eye and draws my attention away from Lang. The lurches and twitches of the sailor-figures have become even more erratic. One lifts an arm in front of its blank wooden face and drops it again, repeating the motion in a juddering staccato. I stare, caught in the sudden notion that it is trying to communicate something, that it is waving to me. Then an even worse explanation strikes me.

"Lieutenant Lang," I call and stand up from my cold seat.

He turns, frowning. At his back, the lake shore is still a fearfully long distance away.

"I think the spring is winding down," I say.

His frown deepens. He mutters under his breath again, probably the sort of thing that young ladies are never supposed to hear, and grips the rail of the ship with both hands. The wind kicks up harder, sending pink spray flying across the deck.

I look away from his dark eyes and back to the juddering sailor-figures. Atop the mast, the wooden bird lifts its wings, then lets them fall with a jerk. Each time it moves with more agonizing slowness, my heart sinks.

Winding the spring again is out of the question. What was a simple motion when the ship fit into my cupped palms will be all but impossible now that the ship has become large, or we have become miniature. I'm not sure which way it is, but in any case, the winding mechanism is also at the bottom of the ship, underwater.

With a last shudder, the sailor-figures and the bird on the mast fall still. Only the sail continues moving, flapping wildly as the ship stops its forward motion.

Another terrible thought occurs to me: the winding mechanism and the wheels are set directly into the hull of the ship. There is nothing watertight about this vessel. It was never meant to actually take to the water. If whatever was keeping it moving forward has failed, then it probably will sink next. I'll never bring Clara home. I may not make it back myself.

"This is less than ideal," Lang says.

His wry humor must be infecting me, because I immediately reply, "I didn't exactly have 'drown in rose water' on my dance card, Lieutenant."

It's enough to make him smile, at least momentarily. "I hate to disappoint a lady," he says.

He didn't hesitate to disappoint me this morning, when I couldn't stop him from dueling with the nutcracker. That was before he took an oath to protect and assist me, however. "You have a plan for our salvation, then?" Now would be an excellent time for him to demonstrate some impressive spell.

"Do you know anything about sailing?" he asks.

"No," I say. "This is the largest ship I've ever been on." It's also the only ship I've ever been on. I don't think the swan-pulled chariot that carried me across this lake before really counts as a ship. It was more of a large pink seashell, and it had no sails.

"And what about swimming?" he says as I move past the useless sailor-figures to stand next to him.

"Can't you sail the ship?" I ask.

Lang shakes his head. "I've never had a reason to learn. The wind will push us as far as it pleases, and I can keep us afloat for a while longer, but there's a cost."

Now that I'm closer to him, I can see a sheen of sweat on his brow despite the cold wind. He's paying some cost already, while I'm standing around like a useless doll. I can swim a little, but my layered winter clothing will probably drag me down to the depths of the lake long before I can make it to shore, especially as tired as I feel. There must be something else I can do to avoid ending up in the water.

I scramble back to where the sailor-figures have stopped trying to catch the flying ropes. If I can tame the sail, then the wind can help us instead of merely pulling all the warmth from my body. I grab the bottom edge of the sail and work my way, hand over hand, toward one corner, until I can grab the line there. It bucks and twists like a live thing, threatening to pull out of my grasp as soon as I have it.

There should be something to secure it to, but when I look around, the sides of the ship are smooth brass and there is nothing on the deck except for the sailor-figures. Perhaps the finished clockwork Godfather made for the king's table had more of the fittings a real ship should have, but this one does not. The only option is to lash it to the sailor-figure. I mutter an apology and make an extremely inelegant knot around the figure's outstretched wrist, then go to the other side.

The second rope is more unruly than the first. Now that part of the sail is fixed in place, the wind billows the canvas, then spills over and sends the sail flapping again with even greater force. It takes me three tries before I can wrap it around my hand and forearm. Once I have it, the force of the wind caught in the sail threatens to lift me from my feet.

The other sailor-figure is too far away to use as a fastening point. Instead, there is only me, with the rope around one arm and the other clamped over the brass rail that makes the edge of the ship. The pink water surges and froths around us. I sit down to avoid tumbling overboard. The ship groans as the sail pulls taut and we pick up forward speed.

In the bow, Lang has both hands on the brass rail, his grip so tight that his knuckles have gone white. He looks up at the sail belling out over his head, and then back over his shoulder at me. "Excellent work, Mademoiselle Stahlbaum," he calls. "Now let us hope we can both hold on long enough."

ELEVEN

I LEAN into the cold brass side of the clockwork ship. The continual spray of rose water coming over the rail has me half-soaked, and soon the wet rope rubs and chafes the bare hand I have wrapped it around. If I try to switch my grip, though, I'm afraid the wind will tear the rope away and I don't know if I have the strength to catch the sail again.

Lang stands at the bow, his own hands still gripping hard on the rail of the ship as he continues whatever he's doing to hold us above the water. The ship is moving forward at a good clip now, and the forms of the swans are becoming more distinct against the slice of dark shore visible to me below the sail and above the edge of the ship. There's the occasional curve of a long, regal neck, and once I think I catch a glint of the golden necklaces I know they wear.

Aren't they cold, in the water and the wind? But they are wild creatures cloaked in sleek oiled feathers and warm down, while I am a woman, wrapped in wet wool and achingly far from home as the sky grows dark above us. I can't feel my fingers anymore, and I don't know how much longer I'll be able to hold on to the rope. Then again, I'm so frozen and cramped, perhaps I couldn't let go if I tried.

I blink my eyes, wet from wind-pulled tears and the flying spray, and focus on the swans. A few more have lifted their heads from under their wings. The groans and creaks the brass ship is making must carry across the water to the birds, disturbing their sleep. I never suspected that ships were so noisy. A true wooden ship under sail must rustle and moan like a forest in a gale, or maybe this one is particularly loud with the wet, bubbling rush of water through the gears below the deck.

I look across to the poor blank-faced figure to whom I tied the other rope. It shivers with the same strain I'm feeling, holding the sail and the wind in check. What a strange thing a sail is, that seeks to tame the wind and steal its power. The idea of sailing suddenly feels as implausible as the existence of the Kingdom of Dolls.

Before my mind can wander too far down that path, however, there is a sudden wrenching crack.

The sailor-figure's arm rips from its body at the shoulder and flies through the air. The wind sends the sail flapping madly again, and the other rope jerks my arm so viciously that it feels as if I'm being ripped apart, too.

Lang turns at my scream of pain, just in time to duck the flying chunk of wood that was the sailor-figure's arm. It knocks his shako from his head and sends it spinning away into the water. If he'd been standing up straight, it would have struck his skull. He lifts his hands to touch his newly bare head. Our gazes meet across the water-slick deck, and I know we are both thinking what might have been.

Then the ship makes a different sound: an odd gurgling, audible even over the rushing wind and waves. Lang's eyes widen, and he slaps his hands back onto the rail, but it's too late. Whatever he'd been doing to keep us afloat is broken, and now we are sinking.

The ship gurgles again. I take a few gasping breaths against the pain in my shoulder before I can unclench my other arm from the rail and start to disentangle myself from the ropes. My fingers are stiff and my legs are no better when I stand up and move carefully to the prow of the ship where Lang is, trying to avoid the flapping sail and not jar my shoulder.

"Now what?" I ask as I reach his side.

"Now you answer my question about whether you can swim," he says.

The sail dances around us, and we are in twilight now. I can't tell how far the shore is or how deep the water is. In the low light, the color of the lake seems darker and more akin to blood than blossoms.

"I can swim," I say, for what other choice do I have? I don't want to end this adventure at the bottom of the lake, where I will be no help to Clara or anyone else. We're closer to shore than when we started. It will have to be close enough.

I fumble at the fastenings of my coat with numb fingers. I won't be able to swim at all with the heavy wool weighing me down, but if I can remove it, I might have a chance of making the shore. We'll find some place to get warm, and then we'll start on the search for Clara and the nutcracker.

My shoulder is painful, and my hands are clumsy with cold. I only manage a few buttons before Lang stops me and points out over the water.

"Look," he says.

I look, and there, flying through the darkness on wide shining wings, is the flock of swans. I stare with my mouth wide open. As a child, all things were large to me, and I hadn't realized how huge they really are. They are as big as horses or cattle, each wing as large as the sail beside me.

They approach us, then circle downward in a wide, curving spiral. There are a dozen of them. They land in the pink waves like dollops of whipped cream, and float there, shimmering in the lavender-gray dusk. They still have their golden necklaces, and their necks curve gracefully as they move their heads this way and that to look at us from different angles.

All the while, they are trading bell-like calls back and forth. It's a lovely, lively sound, much more musical than the swans at home. I want to sit down to listen to their calls and to stare at their wild elegance, but cold water slops over my feet and reminds me of our present predicament.

I turn to Lang, who is staring at the swans in equal wonderment. "Lieutenant Lang," I say, "the ship is sinking."

"I am aware," he says. "Hush."

I have no intention of drowning quietly, though it does seem a shame that my piteous cries will disrupt the music of the swans' calls. "Lieutenant," I start again, but he makes one of those swift, startling movements he is capable of and places a finger over my lips to silence me.

Instinctively, I place my hand over his to pull it away. His hands are also bare, but somehow he is still warm, which hardly seems fair.

"They are discussing you," he says before I can speak. "They remember you."

That silences me, and I let go of his hand.

The ship makes another unhappy gurgle. I look away from the swans, only to see pink water fountaining up through the deck along the two tracks set for the movements of the sailor-figures. We don't have time to listen in on the swans' conversation. We need to get off this ship before it sinks under the surface of the rose water lake and pulls us with it.

Before I can start arguing with him, Lang speaks to the swans. "Forgive a poor traveler's rudeness, Your Excellencies," he calls.

They cease their noise and turn their attention to him. The ones at the back of the flock stretch their long necks to see.

"I find myself in a difficult position, as I have not your facility for travel over water and I must see this young lady safely to shore, for she is under my protection."

The swans begin calling again, all of them speaking at once to judge by the noise. The nearest one leans its head in close, peering first at me, then at Lang, with bright, dark eyes. The necklace it wears is made of large, jointed placards of gold. Each piece shifts with the swan's movements.

"Your Excellency," I say, following Lang's lead and addressing the swan as politely as I know how. "I apologize for coming before you in such a state. I would be much gratified if you could find some way to assist us in reaching dry land."

It still looks at me, as if it expects something else, so I reach into my pocket. I have no marzipan, but I do have the bread I couldn't bring myself to eat earlier. It's not even terribly wet, having been protected beneath my coat. I unwrap it from my handkerchief and hold it out, keeping my hand flat, as if I were offering a treat to a horse. The swan inclines its head to consider the offering. It nibbles once, then takes the whole chunk without grazing my skin and swallows it before calling to its fellows.

"Very good," Lang says softly to me. "That was the right thing, I think." He tilts his head to one side and nods as the swan turns back to us and lets out another musical call. "We shall be eternally grateful to Your Excellencies," he says graciously to the swans, then to me he says, "With your permission, Mademoiselle Stahlbaum?"

"Yes," I say, although I can't understand the swans and don't know what I'm permitting. Anything other than drowning, though, has my wholehearted approval. The water is past my ankles, and my feet are as numb as my hands. I hope the swans will take us somewhere safe and dry because I don't think I'd actually be able to swim anywhere when my limbs already feel like blocks of wood.

Lang extends his hand and indicates that I should step up onto the rail. I clamber up unsteadily, leaning my weight against him to avoid making any movement with my wrenched shoulder. He places a hand at my waist to steady me. The swan bobs closer.

"Am I to…?" I let the question trail off, not sure what is expected of me.

The swan makes an encouraging trill, and Lang nods. "His Excellency asks that you seat yourself on his back."

I cling to Lang's hand and step across from the boat onto the stiff white feathers between the swan's wings. As soon as I can, I sit down. I'm not sure I could hold on to any part of the swan even if it didn't seem rude to try, so I just fold myself up as much as I can.

The pink water of the lake is much closer than it was from the ship. My stomach lurches, but the swan is surprisingly steady, and its folded wings give me some protection from the wind. It twists its head around to look at me and makes another gentle trill.

"Are you comfortable?" Lang asks.

I can't tell if he's translating or asking out of politeness on his own account, but I nod and say, "I am as well as may be, thank you."

My swan moves away from the side of the ship, and another comes forward to take Lang. As he steps off the rail, the ship begins to cant over to one side. My swan glides further from the clockwork ship. The sailor-figures are forlorn shadows on the tilted deck beneath the flapping sail.

The swan with Lang comes beside mine, and the rest of the flock circles around us. What do they see when they look at us through the dusk? I'm a mess: bare-headed and bare-handed, wet through, and with my injured arm tucked close to my body like a broken wing. If my mother and Luise could see me now, they would be horrified. I'm just glad to avoid drowning.

The swans finish their inspection, and we start toward the shore. I look back to the brass ship, receding behind us. The water is over the rail, sloshing back and forth around the waists of the doomed sailor-figures. I whisper a few words of gratitude for their service. They did what they were designed to do; it's not their fault they found themselves on a lake rather than a banquet table.

I look back one last time, searching for the wooden sea bird that topped the mast, but the brass ship is gone. I turn forward. It's nearly dark now, and I can't make out much of what awaits us. Ahead is the shore of the lake, the blackness of the snow-dusted forest, and, somewhere still further off, Clara.

TWELVE

THE swans carry us across the lake while the wind buffets around us. I crouch as low as I can and try not to think of the cold water, or the faceless sailor-figures sinking below its surface. Then, abruptly, the wind stops. We are in a small cove, and the outstretched arms of land welcome us onto the beach.

The swans continue swimming until the water is shallow enough that they walk right up onto the shore. My swan curves its great head around and nudges me gently until I put my good hand on its neck to steady myself. Its feathers are as slick as satin under my touch, but I can feel the sinuous power of the muscle beneath them. If the swans took a dislike to anyone, they could do a good deal of damage.

"Thank you, Your Excellency," I say. I half-step, half-slide down over its wide wing and land on round pebbles that shift under my feet. Dry land, at last. I reach down and spread out my fingers, just so I can touch it. The beach isn't actually dry, of course, but it is reassuringly solid. I pick up one of the damp pebbles, and it's smooth and comfortable in the hollow of my palm.

Lang has disembarked as well. The swans ring around him as he thanks them with effusive politeness. "Are we far from the capital?" he asks. "We are looking for someone who has recently arrived there."

The swans reply in their musical tones. I can understand only half of the conversation that follows, but it seems that we're still some distance away and the swans know nothing of Clärchen. My heart sinks. I remind myself that the swans live here on the lake, so what happens in the capital must be slow to reach them, if it reaches them at all. Just because they haven't heard of Clara's arrival doesn't mean that she isn't there.

Lang asks them about the lake and the land around it, and soon the whole flock has focused on him. I'm on the outside, in the chill dark, but I find that I don't care. I'm so tired that I don't think I can stay standing much longer, let alone put together the type of formal, courtly phrases that Lang is using with the swans.

I walk up the beach and away from the flock, moving slowly as the pebbles shift beneath me. When I find a large, fallen log in front of me, I use the last of my energy to clamber on top of it.

The log is as wide as a table. Wind and water have smoothed away its bark, and it feels almost soft beneath my hands. Can I not just stretch myself out and sleep here? The wind has disappeared, along with the light. The sounds the swans make are musical and soothing, and I am so very tired. I have no idea how many hours have passed since I woke before dawn, but it feels like years since Trudy and I hurried outside the city wall.

This is all my fault. I should have done more to stop the duel between Lang and Drosselmeier. If I hadn't told the nutcracker I didn't want to go into his kingdom, he wouldn't have taken Clara in my place. If I hadn't disrupted the fight by throwing my mittens at Lang, he would've killed Drosselmeier and none of us would be in the Kingdom of Dolls. If I hadn't let Lang provoke me, if I hadn't said that I loved the nutcracker, then Drosselmeier would not have been released from the curse. Or, if Lang hadn't forced the nutcracker into a duel, I would've had time to talk with him and convince him to take a more reasonable course of action.

I lean over and pillow my head on my uninjured arm. There's no point to spinning circles in what has already happened. It won't get Clara back. There is nothing I can do to change the past, and right now there's little I can do for the future either. I just need to rest a little, and then we'll get on with finding Clara and the nutcracker.

I close my eyes and hope my mother isn't worrying too much about me. I hope Fritz will tell her and Luise that Clara and I will be back home soon. I hope we reach the capital in the morning and learn that the nutcracker came and went and never had Clara with him, because I hope that Clara has been found at home with Luise.

I fall into a doze, imagining how I'll tell her the story of my adventure when we are both home. She'll be tucked snugly in her own little bed, looking up at me with wide eyes as I tell her about riding on the swans. I can almost see the glow of the lamps and feel the warmth of the fire when Lang's voice intrudes. "Mademoiselle Stahlbaum," he says, "you must not sleep."

The cozy vision disappears as he sets his hands on my shoulders and pulls me upright. Pain slices through my wrenched shoulder, and tears come to my eyes.

I glare wetly at him, trying to find the details of his face in the twilight. "Go away," I say. "Leave me alone."

"You're cold and wet," he says brusquely, as if I don't know it already.

"I'm tired," I say and try to lie down again.

"You can't sleep like this," Lang says. "And not in this place, either."

I try to push him away, but all I accomplish with my struggle is to send fresh pain shooting through my abused shoulder.

How dare he wake me up? How dare he keep me from my

dream of a warm, comfortable bedchamber? How dare he try to tell me what to do? I shouldn't be surprised. What has Dietrich Lang done since we met, but spoil everything?

As a mouse, he chewed up all my gingerbread dolls and marzipan figures in the middle of the night. He even threatened to gnaw on my picture books until the nutcracker stopped him. Then he came back as a man and ruined my mother's Christmas Eve party. He bullied me into dancing with him and bullied the nutcracker into a duel—that's all he is, really, a great interfering bully.

"Go away," I say again. I ball my good hand into a fist and pound it against his chest. "I hate you."

"And well you may," he says, ignoring my feeble blows, "but you are under my protection, and I won't let you die of exposure in the night."

Behind him, the pitch of the swans' calling increases momentarily. If I could understand their speech, I'd ask them to peck Lang apart and fly me to wherever Clara is.

But they don't know where she is, and probably the credit for a bit of bread doesn't extend so far. I am cold and wet and trapped on this beach by the dark and my own ignorance. Lang is right. If I sleep, I'll die here in this strange land without having made any progress at all. I'll never find Clara or see my family again. My anger flickers out, and I begin to cry instead.

Now that I'm no longer fighting him, Lang lets go of my shoulders. The energy that accompanied my outburst is exhausted, so I merely sit with tears rolling down my face as he kneels before me to undo my sodden boots. I'm so numb that I barely feel what he's doing, and I can hardly see in the gloom either. The swans are restless white shapes behind Lang.

He finishes with my boots, then stands and makes short work of the buttons on my coat. He presses it open and peels it down from my arms, stopping only when I hiss in pain.

"What is it?" he asks.

I want to lie and say something about my modesty and a strange man removing my clothing, but I can't find the properly cutting words. "My right shoulder," I say reluctantly.

He runs his hands over me, feeling the injured place, and makes a muttered sound of disapproval. "It's out of the socket," he says. "This will hurt."

That's all the warning I have before he wraps one arm around me and pulls at my shoulder. I scream. The swans return my cry in loud, discordant calls. A few of them flap their wings, the stiff rustle of their feathers unexpectedly loud now that the wind has left us.

"It had to be done," Lang says loudly, "or it wouldn't heal." More gently he says to me, "I'm sorry."

I wipe my tears with my other hand. Even in the dark, I can feel his eyes on me. Whatever he did has corrected some of the wrongness I felt in the joint, but it still hurts, and he could've at least said what he was about to do. I want to rage at him again, but it would take too much effort. Instead, I pull my feet up onto the log so I can turn away from him. "Leave me alone," I say.

The pebbled beach shifts and crunches wetly at my back. He is gone. I curl in on myself, trying to wrap my good arm around my ribs and hold in some warmth. I should put my coat back on, but I'm not sure I can. Everything has gone so impossibly wrong. How did I ever think I could rescue Clara on my own when I am defeated so easily?

Something bumps my back. At first, I only scrunch myself up tighter, but the touch comes again, gentle but insistent. I lift my head and look behind me.

It's one of the swans, a huge white ghost in the night. And Lang, because of course he didn't go anywhere. He's still here, standing beside the bird.

The swan makes a low thrumming sound, like plucking the lowest string of a cello, and nudges me with its beak again.

"Her Excellency offers the use of a nest for the night," Lang says. When I don't reply, he adds, "It will be warm."

Warm. Warm is important. "Very well," I say. I turn toward the swan. "Is it far?" I'm not sure how far I'll be able to walk.

"I will take you," Lang says. He steps close again, slides an arm beneath my knees, and lifts me from the log.

"What are you doing?" I ask, even as I find myself putting my arms around his neck for stability. "I just told you I hate you."

"I gave my word to look after you," he replies. "So that is what I'm doing."

His word—as if he were a gentleman, when I know he is nothing of the sort. I almost say it aloud, before I remember that I took his word in the workshop. We each swore an oath to help the other through the Kingdom of Dolls. He's keeping up his end of the bargain when he could very well toss me back into the lake and walk away. In his position, I'd probably be tempted to do just that.

I keep my mouth shut, then close my eyes as well. Lang is sure-footed on the shifting pebbles, following the swan to wherever we're going. Cradled against his warm chest, I fall into something like sleep.

The next thing I know, he's setting me down, and there is a smooth, warm floor beneath me. I sit and blink up at him.

"You can sleep safely here," he says.

"What about you?" I ask.

"I'll be all right," Lang says. "Sleep. Working the magic to bring us here took energy from you, and you need to rest. You'll feel better in the morning."

If he's not going to stay here, I should ask him where he's going, but when I open my mouth, it's on a yawn. The tide of sleep is pulling me down, as inescapable as the way the lake swallowed the brass ship. And Lang can take care of himself. Fritz told me so.

I lie back carefully and see the pale form of a swan hovering above me. It moves its head in a way I can't parse until I feel something soft drifting down onto me.

Feathers. The swan is pulling the down from its own breast to cover me.

More white shapes circle around me, and I have the sense of their long necks bending. The swans drop their soft feathers on me, until I'm covered in a thick drift of down. The feathers have the warmth of the swans' bodies in them, like having the coverlet warmed by a hot brick before you climb into bed. I snuggle into them and fall asleep.

THIRTEEN

W HEN I wake, I'm curled as tight as a chick in an egg, with my feet tucked under my skirts. For several minutes, I stay exactly as I am, keeping my eyes pressed closed and my arms tucked between my knees and my body. I can hear the gentle lap of water all around me, but I am blissfully dry and warm. When I cautiously straighten my legs, something soft tickles against my bare feet.

The swans' down. The nest. The lake. The clockwork ship and the wooden sailors and Lieutenant Lang.

I open my eyes and sit up quickly, but I am alone. Lang is not here, and neither are the swans.

I look around, brushing feathers from my face. The nest is a circular space of smooth, dry mud bordered with pressed grass and twigs and walled all around by tall rushes. The circle of sky above me is the cold, pearly gray of early morning, speckled with small high clouds.

I reach out to feel the edges of the nest, and the movement lets me know how stiff my entire body is. My shoulder, at least, doesn't feel much worse than any other part of me. I have Lang to thank for that, I suppose, as well as for negotiating with the swans and bringing me here.

Where is here, though? And where is Lang? I remember being very angry with him last night, but now I'm not sure what about.

I sit for another few minutes, slowly working the kinks from my muscles. My skirts are crumpled, and my petticoats are faintly pink around the hems. My feet are bare, which means that Lang removed my wet stockings as well as my boots last night. I can remember the warmth of his body, too, as he carried me to this nest, but he's not here now.

I undo my hair and comb it as best as I can with my fingers, but my thoughts keep circling back to Dietrich Lang. What if he had slept beside me in this bed of feathers? I pluck a bit of white down from my hair and twirl it in my fingers. It would be warmer, and nothing more. He's only using me to get to the nut-cracker, and if he's left me behind now, it's because I told him to leave. Oh, and—for my memory of last night is filling in—that I hate him.

I wince as I remember the words. No wonder I'm all alone now. He's probably gone to the capital by himself to hunt down the nutcracker. I'll have to hurry if I'm to catch up to him and get Clara away before she ends up witnessing what will probably be Herr Drosselmeier's bloody final moments.

I braid my hair into a crown around my head and stand up in the nest. It's on a small island, surrounded by water. The water is no barrier to a swan, of course, and Lang must have waded through it last night to bring me here. I'll have to do the same to leave. At least the shore isn't far.

I take a last look around the swan's nest and the cloud of down that made my bed, then I climb through the rushes that surround the nest. They turn out to be licorice whips, instead of the plants I would find at home. With everything else, I'd almost forgotten the nature of this place, where things are just as likely to be made of sugar as they are to be wood or stone or living flesh.

I hike up my skirts around my thighs and step down from the edge of the nest into the pink water. It's cold enough that it stings my skin. I think of Clara, grit my teeth, and step away from the island.

Lang was supposed to help me find my niece, but now he's gone and I'm the only one who can help her. I want to hurry to shore, but I force myself to step carefully. Right now, my clothes are dry, and my sore shoulder is my only injury. If I turn my ankle and fall in the water, though, then I might as well lie down in the lake and let whatever passes for fish here nibble on my useless bones.

The thought triggers a memory from my first visit: little children pulling hazelnuts from the lake's rosy water on their fishing lines. My stomach grumbles. I could definitely eat a hazelnut the size of a lake trout right now, but I have little idea how to fish in my own world, let alone here. What bait does one use to tempt a hazelnut to bite a hook?

These ruminations keep my mind busy long enough for me to reach the shore, where I find my coat, stockings, and boots spread in a neat line along the massive log where I nearly fell asleep last night. I carefully thread my arms back into the coat, pull it around me, then turn to the process of covering my feet.

A sharp vibration of wings slices through the air above me. I stop trying to lace my stiff boots and look up as a hawk passes overhead. It flies low enough that I have the brief impression it is looking at me, eye to eye. Probably it has never seen such a miserable, draggled creature as I am right now.

I envy its simple animal elegance. If only I had wings to fly across this land!

The hawk disappears somewhere inland. I finish with my boots and slowly button up my coat. The thick wool is still slightly damp, but it's better than nothing.

In the clear morning air, the towers of the capital are visible where the shore of the lake curves. I can walk there by midday if I find a path to follow, but I won't get far if I don't find some food. Everything around me, of course, is made of edible things, but I find myself reluctant to eat the landscape. It seems rude, and possibly dangerous. If everything here is created by magic, will it even fill my belly? Perhaps I shouldn't have given away my bread to the swan—but I needed its help, and such favors can't go unpaid.

I start walking. The wind off the lake has scoured away the snow and drifted it up on the far side of a wide meadow, which is full of sparkling colored candies on tall stalks, strange flowers untouched by the cold.

My stomach twinges. It seems an age since I sat in God-father's workshop, nibbling at old cheese and shriveled apples. Fritz, my practical brother, eats whatever is placed in front of him, whatever the hour. I should have taken his example.

I ignore my hunger as long as I can, but eventually I pluck one of the candies. It comes away as easily as picking a flower. When I pop it into my mouth, nothing terrible happens except that it is lemon-flavored. I shouldn't have taken a yellow one. I've never been fond of lemon.

I roll the candy around my tongue until it's gone and I'm stepping into a grove of trees where the white boughs are coated with frost, or perhaps with sugar. Silver and golden fruits hang in the branches, paper-wrapped like the apples on our Christmas tree. I pull one down and find that it unwraps to reveal a perfectly ripe pear.

I'm eating my fourth pear when I suddenly know I am not alone in the forest. There is a small noise: a rustle of pine nee-dles, perhaps, or the slump of sugar-snow sliding heavily from a branch.

The moment after I hear it, I can't recall the sound, only that there was one. A shiver runs over my skin as I turn slowly in place, trying to see through the gathered branches of the trees. All is white and green, shot through with glimpses of silver and gold.

At home, I would fear wild animals in a forest such as this. A grumbling bear wandering out of its winter sleep, a sly wild cat stalking me, the disagreeable bulk of a wild boar taking exception to me in its territory. I remember the nutcracker's tale of the giant Leckermaul attacking his castle. Would such a monster attack me, or would it be satisfied with the edible scenery? Whatever predators this land has, all I have to defend myself with is a half-eaten pear. Where the devil is Lang, with his saber and his oath to protect me? He is exactly the sort to take on a rampaging giant. I should have been more polite to him instead of sending him away.

I shift the fruit in my grip, readying it for throwing. There is a crunch of footsteps in the snow, and my heart flutters and twists like a flock of sparrows frightened up into the sky. I raise the pear, then hesitate, wondering if such a paltry missile will only enrage whatever is moving through the forest toward me. Should I run instead?

In this pause, my eye finally catches the movement in the trees. The shape resolves into a dark green uniform, nearly the same shade as the pine boughs, except for the flashes of gold braid. I let out the breath I've been holding as Lang stalks through the trees to stand before me. Not a predator—or at least, not an unknown one.

"Mademoiselle Stahlbaum," he says. "I expected you would wait for my return."

"I didn't know you were coming back," I say.

Lieutenant Lang steps closer. I can see the dusting of white crystals in his hair, sparkling on his eyebrows and even his eyelashes. He looks very much like a creature of magic.

He also looks deeply annoyed.

"I left you safe and warm and sleeping," he says. "You were supposed to stay there. Instead, I must track you through the forest."

"I could have stayed safe and warm at home, Lieutenant Lang," I say. I meant to apologize, but he hasn't bothered to say 'Good morning,' or 'Sorry for frightening you,' or even, 'I've found your niece and we can all go home now.' My body is still shaking with the potent mix of fear and relief he's just caused, and now I'm annoyed, too. "How was I to know you'd come back?" I ask. "You didn't exactly leave a note."

"What would I have left a note on?" he returns.

I don't throw the pear. Instead, I toss the crumpled ball of silver paper from my other hand at him.

He catches it without even looking, which only makes me angrier. My shoulder still hurts, my feet are cold again, and I know my clothes are beyond wrinkled after I slept in them wet. Despite my best efforts at finger-combing, I probably still have feathers in my hair. Meanwhile, Lang appears as fresh as when he walked into our Christmas Eve party. If he hadn't already told me that he studied arcane magics, I would suspect it now.

"Perhaps you could've used a spell," I say. "Don't you know any useful magics?"

"I kept you from drowning yesterday," he says tightly. "Is that not useful enough?"

He glares at me. I glare back and consider that this might be the moment to throw the pear at him, since I don't have a good reply. He would probably swat it away without noticing, however, so I don't. I take a deep breath and remind myself that I'm not here to spar with Lang, I'm here to find Clara. A second breath, and I'm able to say calmly, "Thank you for not letting me drown. Or freeze."

He opens his mouth, and I can see that he was ready to respond with more sharp words, but he holds them back at the last moment. "You're welcome," he says instead.

There. We can both be polite, and now we can get on with the search for Clärchen—but we can't. I can't leave it at only being half-polite. I have to say something more, because he did save me yesterday, several times over, and I was far less than grateful. "And," I add, "I apologize for what I said yesterday."

He raises an eyebrow. "Do you mean to say that you do not hate me, Mademoiselle?"

I can feel my cheeks heating. I want to look away from his dark eyes, but I don't let myself. "No, Lieutenant," I say lightly. "I hope I didn't wound you too deeply."

He shakes his head and chuckles, and the warmth on my face spreads through my entire body. But then his expression turns serious again as he looks at me. "I must also apologize, Mademoiselle Stahlbaum," he says slowly. "I have been thinking of you as a pawn in the game, when you are also a player."

This time, I can't hold his gaze. I look down at the half-eaten pear in my hand. "Yes, well," I say, "now that's settled, and we can continue to the capital."

"Yes," Lang says, but he doesn't move.

The silence of the snowy forest pools around us like treacle as I look at him through my lashes, trying to read what he is thinking and failing. I can, at least, see past the glamor of the snow still dusting him now. There are dark smudges beneath his eyes, as if he hasn't slept since he left me in the swan's nest. What has he been doing? The thought of what it might have been to curl our bodies together in the bed of down creeps into my mind again.

Rather than dwell on that, I open my mouth. "I didn't mean to send you away. Not really. I was just so tired. And I would have waited for you to return, but when I woke up, I was hungry. 'Safe' and 'warm' aren't worth much when balanced against 'starving.'"

I take a large bite of pear to illustrate my words. The juice immediately runs down my chin, and I have to wipe it away with the back of my hand, which spoils the effect.

Lang watches as I try to lick the juice from my fingers. Our eyes meet, and this time Lang is the one who looks away. Color creeps up his cheeks, already shadowed by a day's growth of beard. Perhaps he's embarrassed on my behalf. He's the one who was born an animal, yet now I'm the one foraging in the forest like a wild beast.

I pull out my handkerchief, but it is damp and pink with rose water, which only increases my frustration. Despite my claims to the contrary, there is definitely a part of me wishing to be safe and comfortable at home, with a fire in the grate, water in a washbasin, and clean clothes waiting for me.

I stuff the crumpled handkerchief back into my pocket and bend down to scoop up a handful of snow instead. Fortunately, it really is snow: simple, frozen water, and not sugar. I scrub my hands with the granules, and when I straighten, Lang is holding out his own handkerchief.

I unfold the clean white square. It is unembroidered. There is no decorative border, no initials on the corner.

The unworked bit of cloth strikes me in a way that his story hasn't. Dietrich Lang is utterly alone in the world. He has no mother, no sister, no wife—no one who would take the time to add such embellishments to the fabric. All he has to connect him with his family are the circlets on his fingers. No wonder he wanted them back.

I dry my hands and tuck the handkerchief into my pocket. I'm not as skilled with a needle as Luise, but I'm not incompetent. I can't change the past or revive his murdered family, but I can add some embroidery before I return it to him.

FOURTEEN

W̲ᴇ walk through the forest for a quarter of an hour before
I work myself up to break the silence. I consider the questions I
could ask of Lang: entirely inane ones like, 'Do you like pears?'
and wildly inappropriate ones like, 'Did you see your brothers
die, or just your mother?' What I actually ask is, "Why did you
join the army?"

Lang pauses, his hand on the snowy branch he's holding out
of my way. Not until I've passed, and he's let it swing back into
place, does he reply.

"I knew I had to learn to fight. And the Grand Army takes
all volunteers." He takes the lead on the narrow trail we are
following through the trees. At the next place where the spreading boughs cover the path, he again pulls one aside for me, so it
drops the snow onto the ground instead of down my collar. "I
suppose if I hadn't heard so much of your brother ordering his
toy soldiers into battle," he says, "I might have chosen a different path."

"When—" I start to ask, then I realize the answer for
myself. "After the nutcracker wounded you."

He lay alone in the walls of our house, recovering his
strength and listening to our conversations.

Lang nods. "I didn't try to buy a commission as a mouse," he says. "I realized I needed human form to get what I wanted. That was the first thing I set out to do when I had healed. The army was after."

"But you said the astrologer would not reverse the spell," I say. "And that your brothers couldn't find a solution."

"They didn't have time to find it," Lang says, and the flat tone of his voice suggests I am straying too close to painful topics.

I press my lips together over my other questions. Why the Grand Army? Does he believe in the ideals of the emperor and the Revolution, or was it all part of his calculations: find Fritz, find me, find young Drosselmeier? What was it like to transform from an animal to a man, however he managed to make it happen? Did he have to discover all the things that infants learn in the first years of life? What road has he traveled to get where he is today?

The air has warmed, and there is no longer snow in the branches of the trees around us. The path has brought us to a more established road. It's wide enough that we can walk side by side, but I have to stretch my legs to keep up with Lang, and he doesn't offer any further conversation.

Without answers about Lang's mysteries, my mind shifts back to worries about what might be happening with Clara and young Drosselmeier. When the nutcracker brought me into the Kingdom of Dolls, he took me on a tour through his lands that ended in his palace. We were about to dine on fruit and confections in a beautiful crystal hall when I woke up in my own bed. But this time it is winter. This time the nutcracker carries the wounds that Lang gave him. How badly hurt is he, really? What if he hasn't been able to take Clara all the way to the palace, but left her alone somewhere in this land? I remember my earlier anxiety of the Leckermaul and wonder again what sorts of dangers exist here. Swamps of syrup to drown in, perhaps, or swarms of flies to devour you. I have Lang, but who will protect Clärchen until we can find her?

I realize I'm touching my collarbone. My fingers are still looking for my missing necklace. Without the necklace, I've been trying to redirect my nerves to a loose thread at the cuff of my coat, but it's not working very well. The way things are going, I might pick out all the stitching by the end of the day, and then I'll look even more ragged than I already do.

The unsettling thoughts have slowed my feet as well, and I've fallen behind. I hurry after Lang. "Do you have my necklace?"

"I have it," he says. He doesn't stop walking.

"I want it back," I say. "You took your brothers' crowns, but I want the chain they were on."

He stops and turns to me. "You took an oath, Mademoiselle Stahlbaum, to assist me in finding Herr Drosselmeier. And yet, now you try to delay me with frivolous requests."

"I'm not trying to delay you," I say. "But it's mine. You have no right to keep it."

His mouth compresses into a thin line beneath his mustache, and he's glaring at me again. All the ground we gained earlier with our mutual politeness and apologies has been lost. I shouldn't have mentioned his brothers, for he looks as hard and angry as he did before the duel. I've been thinking about Clara, but perhaps his thoughts have been focused on his murdered family and the revenge he seeks.

I bite the inside of my lip, wondering what I can say to soften him. I did swear an oath to him, but at the same time, I promised myself I'd find a way to stay his hand.

While I hesitate, Lang undoes a few of the frog fastenings of his attila jacket and produces the chain from a pocket over his breast. "Here," he says, as he pours the golden links into my palm. "Now, can we continue?"

He doesn't wait for an answer, but starts closing up his

jacket as he walks away down the empty road. I curl my fingers around the chain, warm with the heat of his body, and hurry after him.

Half an hour later, we step out of the forest to find the high walls of the capital city before of us. The road continues on through a gate, though it isn't the formal entrance the nutcracker brought me to before. That was made of macaroons and sugared fruits, while this seems to be a simple tradesman's entrance: two massive slabs of hard-baked gingerbread reinforced with bands of boiled toffee and propped open so carts and travelers can easily enter the city.

As soon as we pass through the gate, we are swallowed up into a jostling crowd. It is as busy and crowded within the city as it was quiet and empty in the forest. I press close to Lang as we join the foot traffic, looking down at the boiled sweets that make the cobblestones of the street and not daring to meet anyone's eyes.

There are no shouts of alarm at our presence, however, and my curiosity soon gets the better of me. I raise my eyes and look around. Immediately, I see why no one takes any notice of us. The street is thronged with all manner of personages. Some are as human as myself—or at least as human-seeming as Dietrich Lang—but just as many others are dolls, puppets, and animals.

I see a scaramouche deep in conversation with a white-clad Greek. In the shade of an arcade delicately decorated with sugar icing, a group of elegant Armenian ladies sit laughing together and eating pomegranates while lions lounge at their feet. Black-robed priests walk with Tyroleans, and a bear lumbers beside a girl who looks like nothing more than a china shepherdess come to life. No one in this varied company has a second glance for us.

"Which way do we go?" Lang asks me.

"To the palace," I say, then hesitate, remembering my earlier doubts about the nutcracker. "Or we could ask someone if he is there. If they've seen Clara."

He shakes his head. "And let them send a warning to him that we are coming? No. If we can surprise him, then we should."

"But you asked the swans, didn't you?"

"They weren't in the capital," he says. "And they'd already shown themselves to be friends. We don't have time now to determine who might help us and who might run immediately to our enemy."

The street ahead opens into a little square, paved with more boiled candies in shades of pink and red and brown. In the center of the square stands a tremendous baumkuchen. The tall, hollow cake really does look like a tree in this instance, or perhaps an obelisk, as it towers above the buildings bordering on the square. Around its base are four fountains spouting lemonade, just barely visible through the milling crowd.

There are more people and creatures here, and a simmering sense of expectation in the air that makes my skin prickle. I look around, trying to see what might be unusual, but everything is so fantastical that nothing stands out. Is it the troupe of monkeys climbing up the buildings on the side of the square? Is it the man in a brocaded dressing gown waving his arms and speaking loudly near the fountains? The Chinese emperor mounted on a sinuous dragon? No one is looking especially at any of these, but still there is a hum in the air.

A murmur runs through the throng around us, too quick for me to catch the words of it. I turn to Lang, about to ask if he heard what it is that everyone is waiting for. Then a harlequin in a tattered red, white, and green outfit climbs up onto the rim of one of the fountains and shouts above the clamor of the crowd.

"The confectioner is coming!" the harlequin calls in a ringing voice. "The confectioner is already here, they say!"

All around us, conversations die. The whole crowd is silent. A moment later, they are all speaking at once.

"The confectioner," repeats a voice to my left.

"The baker," says another.

"The pastry chef."

"The maker."

Everyone speaks a different name, but it's clear they all mean the same personage: the one responsible for the creation of this strange realm.

"It must be Drosselmeier," Lang says. "The clockmaker." His hand strays to the hilt of his saber.

"No," I say. "I don't think so." The nutcracker told me that his uncle could never create something like this kingdom, but do I still believe everything he told me? Who else could have made this land if not my godfather, who has brought dolls and clockworks to me every year? We didn't find him in his workshop. He might be here, holding both Clara and the nutcracker in his control.

"He mustn't see you," Lang says. He's come to a decision while I've been wondering what awaits us in the nutcracker's palace. "Me, he will expect, but not you, I think. Or not both of us together." He tugs me through the crowd to the edge of the street.

We find an open space next to a wall of dark-baked gingerbread inlaid with blanched almonds in a floral pattern. Almost as soon as we pause, a martial fanfare of trumpets and drums sounds from the other side of the square. Lang steps forward, facing me and not looking at the growing commotion around the baumkuchen.

"I want to see," I say, but Lang only moves closer, boxing me in against the wall. He's shielding my body from view with his own, but also blocking me from seeing what is happening.

"He will pass, and we will follow," Lang says. "Be patient."

The crowd presses away from us, toward the square. I can only catch glimpses around Lang, mostly other people's backs viewed beneath his arm.

I try to be patient, but it's not in my nature. What if it is the nutcracker after all, or my godfather? What if he has Clara with him and we simply let them pass by? I set my hands on Lang's chest, steadying myself as I strain up on my toes to look over his shoulder. I can feel the rise and fall of his breath beneath my palms, and I am briefly surprised at my boldness. Then, I catch sight of the carriage crossing the square behind a company of janissaries playing brass instruments. The vehicle is all velvet and gold and mother-of-pearl, open for all to see the important personage inside—but it is empty.

Lang bends his head close to mine, as if we are lovers sharing this moment while everyone else is looking the other direction. "Who do you see?" he asks softly. His breath is warm on my skin, another sensation I wish I had the time to fix in my memory and consider more fully when there is leisure to do so.

"No one," I say. I grip the braid of his attila and lean forward. Everyone else is watching the carriage as it crosses the square, and the faces I see are full of reverent awe. They must see something, but what? When I look at the carriage again, it is still empty, without a shadow or a shimmer to indicate anyone on that broad velvet cushion. "There's no one there."

FIFTEEN

LANG glances over his shoulder. When he looks back at me, I know he doesn't see anything in the carriage either.

I expect him to ask me to search my memory again, to see if I can remember any other detail about this mysterious, invisible confectioner. Instead, he takes my hand in his and pulls me down a side street. I can feel the hard lines of the crowns he wears as rings, though I don't dare look down at our linked fingers as we move quickly past buildings made of pastry, finely filigreed with patterns of chocolate or sugar icing. Rising above them, I see the many towers of the pink and pearlescent marzipan castle.

"Come," he says as we round another corner. "We should be in the castle before whatever is in that carriage arrives."

I have to run to keep up with his longer strides. He never hesitates at the intersections, but it's not hard to tell which way to go: the towers of the castle loom above the rest of the buildings. When I was here before, some of the towers were covered in scaffolding and under repair, but there's no longer any sign of the damage the nutcracker told me had been caused by the giant Leckermaul.

A few streets away, I can hear the tumult of the crowd

and the strident music of the military band. We are drawing ahead—a parade never moves quickly.

We pass a neighborhood of pastry houses with roofs of braided bread, a multi-spired church with windows of colored sugar-glass, a collection of market stalls piled with nutmegs and sugar loaves and sugared violets. Then we turn a last corner and enter the wide plaza before the castle. Lang stops short, and I barely avoid crashing into him.

The entire plaza and the wide boulevard opening onto it are thronged with people of all types and nations. My eye catches on the china shepherdess I saw earlier, with her too pale, too smooth face. Like everyone else, she's watching the route the open carriage will take. Obviously, we can't go in through the castle's grand entrance.

"There must be other doors," I say. There will be a side entrance, a place where the servants go. Even an enchanted castle has servants. Last time I saw little pages in the halls, and the princesses were set to prepare food with their own hands: not all is done by magic here.

Lang nods and tugs me in a new direction. He hasn't let go of my hand, and I'm glad. He won't leave me behind this time.

We skirt the edge of the plaza and slip into a narrow alley beside the castle. Almost immediately, however, our path is blocked by a red-jacketed soldier who looks at us with quick alertness. I step close to Lang, who releases my hand and wraps his arm around my shoulders instead. As he does so, the soldier's expression relaxes from suspicion to friendly conspiracy.

"Ah, young love," he says with a grin, and I am immediately blushing with mortification.

Lang tucks me closer against him. "I thought we'd find a quiet spot here," he says, somehow managing to sound rueful and a little embarrassed at being caught.

It's no artifice for me to hide my hot face against his pelisse, thinking of this stranger assuming that I ducked into this narrow passage to be secretly kissed by Dietrich Lang.

Worse, I can quite easily imagine it. We would stand close, as we did when we heard the procession with the carriage approaching, and I would set my hands on the rough braid of his jacket. Instead of standing on my toes to look over his shoulder, I would lift my face to his, and then—

"Go along then," the soldier says with a laugh. "You won't find a better moment to distract a young lady's duenna, and I won't let anyone else come along after you."

"Thank you," Lang says. I can all but hear the wink he must be giving the other man. His hand slips lower, to my waist, and he bends his head to mine to say, "Come along, liebling," into my hair.

Somehow, I make my legs work and we pass the red-coated soldier and his knowing smile. Lang holds me close at his side until we have turned a corner, then he stops and presses me against the wall, just as I have been imagining. My heart stutters like an overwound clockwork as I look up at him.

He smooths my hair back from my face and says, "My apologies, Mademoiselle Stahlbaum, but we must continue this facade a little longer."

My mouth has gone dry, but I manage a little nod.

"I expect our benefactor will want to take a peek at us," he says, speaking in a low voice as he strokes my cheek with the back of his curled fingers. "If we're engaged in lock breaking rather than lovemaking when he does, then he may recall his duties."

I nod again. His words sound reasonable enough, but I'm struggling with the conflict between my rational mind, which knows his touch is a deception, and my irrational body, which is entirely deceived. I look into his eyes, trying to find something I can anchor myself to in the middle of my swirling emotions.

When he blinks, long dark lashes sweep down almost to his cheeks, and I see he bears a second scar. It is a small, pale line across his left cheekbone, hardly more noticeable than the laugh lines around his eyes.

How odd, given all the tragedy of his life, that his face should bear laugh lines. That Dietrich Lang has found opportunities for laughter is a strange and hopeful thing to see.

Again, he strokes my cheek, and though nothing else of our bodies touches, I feel myself going weak-kneed and soft, like a wax figure left in the sun. If he touches me again, he'll leave an imprint that I'll be aware of until the end of my days.

And would that really be so terrible? Perhaps I would like to be marked by Dietrich Lang. Other things have marked me— some visible, like the scars on my arm, some invisible, like the way my parents shook their heads in disbelief at my stories— but few of them have been things I chose for myself. In this moment, however, I want to choose. So, I screw up my courage and ask, "Will you kiss me?"

His hand on my cheek stills, if only briefly. I take another breath, preparing to claim that I mean it only as part of the pantomime. But he nods. "If you wish it," he says.

"Yes," I say, and then there is an awkward moment while I wonder what to do next, and how many other girls he's kissed and how I might compare, and whether or not I will confide this moment to Trudy or Petra later. Fritz wouldn't approve, nor would my mother—but none of them are here. This moment is only me and Dietrich Lang—and perhaps a nosy, red-coated soldier who thinks he's helping young love on its course.

Lang leans closer, so his forehead rests against mine and our breaths mingle. I lift my hands and slide them experimentally up his chest to clasp behind his neck. We stay like this for a few thunderous heartbeats, then he gently lifts my chin. Instinctually, I close my eyes. Our lips meet and part, and I taste him, sweeter than any sugared confection found in this enchanted land. His hand slides to cup the back of my head and I hold tighter to him and we kiss and kiss and kiss.

111

He kisses the way he dances: masterfully. When we part, I am breathless and tingling from head to toe with unfamiliar but pleasant sensation. It's a good thing I have the solid wall at my back and my arms around his neck, or I might simply slide down to the ground.

I look up through my lashes and find that he is smiling at me. It's not the mischievous smile he wore on Christmas Eve, or the wry, hollow expression when he spoke of his past, but something soft, as if he's just seen a butterfly emerge from a cocoon to dry its wings and is surprised and delighted by the tender newness of it.

Just as I start to smile back, a great roar of sound comes from the direction of the plaza. Trumpets and cheers vie for prominence. Lang's face turns serious. "We must get into the castle," he says.

I untwine my arms from him and make a pretense of shaking out my skirts. He's right: we must hurry and find a way into the castle. Even if I know the taste and feel of his mouth now, nothing else has changed. I want to find Clara. Lang wants to find the nutcracker. Still, a delicious thrill runs over me when he takes my hand again.

We continue down the narrow passageway. On one side is a wall of gingerbread, bordered on the ground level with a line of whole almonds. The dark skin of the nuts is scuffed and flaking away to reveal the pale nutmeats inside. On the other side rises the smooth marzipan of the castle, a swirled surface of cream and pink, like rose marble.

After a second turn, we find a door set into the marzipan wall. Lang motions me behind him and draws his saber. With his free hand, he tries the latch. I hold my breath, but it opens easily and there is no one on the other side.

"Everyone must have gone to see the arrival of the confectioner," I whisper to Lang.

"Then we must move quickly, before they return," he says,

and draws me inside.

We pass quickly through a narrow hallway and up a staircase of chocolate bars covered by a runner of brightly patterned gilt paper. At the top is a gallery paneled in red and yellow hard candy, with recessed alcoves holding glittering white statuary carved from sugar loaves.

There are several doorways, but at the far end, I see one opening on the iridescent walls of the crystal hall where the nutcracker and I were entertained by the princesses who called him brother.

"In there," I say to Lang.

He nods and places a finger to his lips. We cross the gallery silently and stop outside the door. After a moment, I hear a murmur of feminine voices from within and strain my senses, trying to tell if Clara is among them. Then another, familiar voice cuts across them. Lang stiffens beside me, and I know he's recognized Godfather Drosselmeier's speech as well. He doesn't say anything as we retreat from the doorway and back across the candy gallery, where he pulls me into one of the other doorways.

Inside is an orangery. Looking around, I see that it is unoccupied. The fruits hanging from the potted trees are crystallized in a thick coating of sugar.

"You stay here," he says softly, leading me toward a bench beside a pot of preserved lemons. "I'll take a closer look."

"You can't leave me behind," I protest. "What if Clara is there?"

"Then I'll come back and tell you in a few minutes," he says. He undoes his pelisse and lays it on the bench. Next, he removes his sword belt and hands it to me, setting my hand on the hilt of his saber. "If anyone comes, draw this with your good arm and pretend you know how to use it."

"I'm coming with you," I say stubbornly.

"No," he says. "I'm going alone. If all goes well, I'll only be gone for a few minutes, and then we will know better what to do next." Before I can object again, he adds, "You swore an oath not to stand in my way when we found Herr Drosselmeier."

I bite my lip. I don't like any of this, but at least if he's leaving his saber with me, I know he won't be running anyone through with it while we are separated. So I nod. "I will wait here," I say, "but I'm coming after you if you're not back in a quarter of an hour."

He gives me his wry smile and touches my cheek for the briefest of moments. "I would expect no less," he says. Then he turns and walks out of the orangery.

The instant he's out the door, I lay the saber down and follow after him. I promised that I would wait, but not that I would stay sitting on the bench like a goose.

I peek out into the gallery and watch Lang as he walks away. Then, between one step and the next, his shape shimmers and shifts. I blink against the seeming haze over my vision. Lang is gone. There is no longer a man in the gallery, but an uncommonly large mouse running across the floor toward the entrance of the crystal hall.

SIXTEEN

I DRAW back and return to the bench in the orangery. My hands are trembling as I sink onto the seat. I clasp them tightly in my lap.

Dietrich Lang is not only a hussar. He is the king of mice. I had nearly forgotten that he was the monster of my childhood. Now, I close my eyes and see again the terrible furry creature crouched in the glow of my bedside lamp, threatening to bite my nutcracker doll in two.

Slowly, I untangle my fingers, take my gold chain from my pocket, and worry the links between my fingers. Beside me, Lang's saber lies across his fur-lined pelisse. If I were to press my fingers into the lining, I would still feel the animal warmth of his body.

I let him kiss me. I asked him to kiss me, and I can still feel the way our mouths pressed together. I lift a hand and run my fingers over my lips, as if I might actually find an indent left there by his touch.

Perhaps everything my family has told me is true. Perhaps I am the one who is mad, lost in a strange fantasy world of my own making. Any moment now, I'll wake up in my bed on Christmas morning, with a head sore from too much spiced wine.

Reality shifts around me, as it did before. No one has ever believed my stories. Next time I see Dietrich Lang in company with my brother, he may join in with those laughing at me for believing in such foolish things as magic and fairy tales.

I wind the gold chain around my left forefinger and pull until it hurts. Does that mean I'm not dreaming, or only that I'm dreaming my finger hurts? I don't know any more.

The tip of my finger turns purplish. How much time has passed? Should I go after Lang? What will I see if I do? Perhaps he's gone to fulfill his long-ago threat to bite the nutcracker in two. I unwind the chain and rub my finger.

There is a whisper of sound in the doorway, and I look up. I can't arrange my face properly before Lang sees me. I don't even know what emotions I ought to be reflecting, but it doesn't matter. The moment our eyes meet, he stops in mid-stride next to the sharp fronds of a pineapple.

"You saw me," he says.

I twist the golden chain through my fingers. I don't bother answering, for what can I say? *Yes, I saw you. I know what you are.* He's not anything different from what he was an hour ago, and yet—

He makes a half-turn, as if he might walk out of the orangery, then abruptly faces me. "You simply cannot do as you are told, can you?" he says bitterly. "I asked you to stay here, and you couldn't do it."

"I didn't leave this room," I say. That was the promise he asked for, and the promise I gave. "I didn't break my word. I waited."

He advances on me with long, predatory strides. *Monster*, whisper my memories. *Man*, say my eyes. My heart twists like an animal in a hunter's snare.

I reach for the saber he left with me and wrap my fingers around the hilt. It's a foolish thing to do. I'm not sure I can actually lift it, let alone cause any deeper damage than dropping it on his foot. Still, when I stand, blade in hand, Lang sees the movement. It stops his feet, if not his mouth.

"If you had only listened to your mother," he says, scowling at me. "If you had only gone to bed when you were told instead of staying late to cosset your dolls, then I would've finished this long ago. The nutcracker would be ended, my mother would be avenged, and you"—he jabs a finger at me—"would be at home with your niece and the rest of your family."

As if I have any responsibility for this situation, when all I've done from the beginning is try to stop them from hurting one another. "Do not lay the blame for this at my feet," I say. "If you hadn't come stirring things up, then Herr Drosselmeier would not have been so desperate as to run and steal Clara away." I hold out his saber. "How is this going to solve any-thing?" I ask. "Men with swords and rifles and cannons have been marching across Europe for my entire life—from Paris to Moscow, from Berlin to Brussels, and back again—and what has it accomplished? Nothing but death and more death."

I uncurl my fingers and let the saber fall. Lang covers the last distance between us and catches it up before it clatters to the floor.

"Do you want us to be discovered?" he asks sharply.

"I want to find Clara," I say. "You are supposed to be help-ing me."

"Do you still trust me to?" he asks.

"I—" But he's cut straight to the heart of the matter, as surely as if he'd drawn the saber and cleaved through the Gor-dian knot of my emotions. Do I trust him? I'm not sure I have ever trusted him, except that I have: I trusted his oath that he would help me, trusted his arms to carry me last night, trusted him to lead me through the capital today, trusted his mouth on mine. "I want to trust you," I say.

"Wanting does not make it so," he says.

"Perhaps this is all a dream," I say desperately. "Perhaps I am dreaming all of this, including you."

"If you have dreamed my life for me," Lang replies, "then I must say that you have an exceedingly cruel imagination, Mademoiselle Stahlbaum."

He has returned to his bitter, empty smile, and I can't find the words to answer him. I don't want to think I have imagined the deaths of his family, but I am unmoored. I want to wake up. At the thought, the potted trees of the orangery seem to shimmer translucently around me.

"If you aren't going to help me, then leave me alone," I say to Lang.

"As the lady wishes," he says. He gives me a stiff bow, then grabs his pelisse and stalks out of the orangery.

I sink down on the bench and place my head in my hands. I should run after Lang, but this time he left with his saber and with anger in every movement of his body. I don't know what he will do next. No, I know exactly what he will do. He will find the nutcracker and kill him.

I press my hands against my eyelids, trying to review everything that has happened and see where I went wrong. Was there anything I could have done to avoid coming to this point? But I can't see any place where I would've acted differently. I had to try to stop the duel. I had to tell young Drosselmeier that I didn't want to go with him. I had to follow him into this realm to find Clara. I had to rely on Lang's help to get this far, or I would've drowned straight away in the lake of rose water yesterday.

Even the kiss I would not change, but what am I to do now? Even if he was soft for that brief moment, now he is hard and sharp again—all teeth and talons and temper. Yesterday, I told him I hated him and he didn't take me seriously because he knew I was cold and tired and out of sorts. He came back for me this morning, but he won't make the same mistake a second time.

"*Snap snip, snip snap!*"

A too-familiar voice interrupts my melancholy thoughts. I lift my head to find Godfather Drosselmeier standing before me.

"*A mouse in the house*
Will soon trip a trap—
Snap! snap! snap! snap!"

I blink at him. Is this another trick of my mind? But he looks as he has always looked, with his yellow frock coat and his spindly old man's legs. His white wig shines like spun glass.

"Mariechen," he says. "I didn't know you had come to play in the Kingdom of Dolls."

I could almost laugh at his words, if I wasn't afraid that it would turn immediately to tears. Nothing of this journey has been so carefree as play. "I came to find Clara," I say. "Where is she?"

Godfather raises his eyebrow. I imagine the other moves in tandem, though it is hidden behind the black silk of his eye patch. "Clara?" he asks. "Why would I know where the child is?" He walks past the potted trees and smiles benevolently down at me.

"What of your nephew?" I ask.

"Ah," Godfather says. "My nephew. That fool jumping jack." He shrugs his shoulders and lifts the tails of his coat to sit beside me on the bench. "He's scratched right down through the paint. Naughty children—always so careless with your toys. He will need to be mended."

"He's not a toy," I say. "He was bleeding. He should have gone to Herr Wendelstern." He will need more than fresh paint to recover from the duel with Lang.

Godfather clucks his tongue in disapproval. "He is yours, Marie. He's under your care, and you let him be broken for a second time. I fixed him for you before. Am I to do it again?"

"But he's not a toy," I repeat. "He is a man." I shift over on the bench, away from where my godfather sits.

"He's a doll I gave to you when you were small, Marie," Godfather says. "Nothing more." He's still smiling, but I don't think he's really listening to what I'm saying.

"You told me he was your nephew," I say. "You told me how he became enchanted after cracking the nut for the princess."

Godfather shakes his head. "Ah, child," he says. "You are dreaming again. You have such a wonderful imagination."

"Then why are you in my dream?" I ask.

"Perhaps it is you who are in my dream," he says slyly. He lifts his hand, and I see that he's holding a little golden key: the one he used to wind the dolls on Christmas Eve. "Perhaps this kingdom is merely another plaything I have created for you."

I shake my head, trying to clear it. Is this one of Godfather's creations? He made us castles. He made the clockwork ship. Did he make the nutcracker? Or Lang?

But my sturdy, practical brother saw Lang, knew him, brought him to our home on Christmas Eve. If he is real to Fritz, then he must be as real as anyone else I know, even if I am in a dream world now. I didn't create him from my imagination, and neither did Godfather Drosselmeier. And if Lang is real, then I have to trust his story about the nutcracker, as he trusted in my story of the Kingdom of Dolls.

"No," I say to my godfather. "This is not your creation. The things you make must be wound, and they can only do what you set them out to do." I think of the silver swans on the lake, the way they came to Lang's and my rescue while Godfather's poor wooden sailors sank with their brass ship. "The residents of this land do not wind down. They make their own choices; they aren't your clockwork dolls."

Godfather scowls at me. "Child," he begins.

"I'm not a child," I interrupt. "And if this is a dream, then it is my dream and you are not welcome in it."

Godfather opens his mouth, but whatever words he's about to say are overtaken by a wide yawn. He blinks in surprise, then lifts his hand to cover his mouth as a second yawn squeezes his good eye shut. His form wavers and grows hazy.

I feel myself blurring, too. The waking world tugs at me, but I wrap the gold chain around my finger and pull until the narrow edges of its links bite into my skin and the pain grounds me. Even if this is a dream, I can't leave now, not without Clara. It was hard enough to get here, and I haven't accomplished any of what I set out to do. "I'm not a child," I say again.

For a third time, my godfather yawns. My ears itch with the instinct to yawn in sympathy, but I fight against it. Godfather Drosselmeier's form is half-transparent now: the shadow of a yellow frock coat and a dark smudge of eye patch. His mouth opens again, to yawn or to try to tell me once more that I do not know my own mind—I can't hear the words anymore.

My own yawn is still fighting to get out. I clench my jaw until my eyes water. My godfather is nothing but a wisp of sickly yellow, and then he is gone. The golden key falls to the floor with a crystalline ting.

SEVENTEEN

I STAND and stare at the bench where Godfather Drosselmeier sat. Is this place my dream? But it cannot be my dream
alone—perhaps I dreamed up the lake and the swans, but not
this castle. As soon as I think it, I know whose dream the beautiful marzipan castle must be: young Drosselmeier's.

A youth who had neither shaved nor worn boots—he was
barely more than a child when his uncle took him to break
the princess's curse. He must have wanted to be the prince
beside the princess he rescued, and when that didn't happen,
he dreamed this castle into being as a place where he could be
a prince in his own right instead of trapped within the wooden
body of the nutcracker doll.

I pick up the golden key that fell to the floor with my godfather's disappearance and tuck it into my coat pocket. As I do so,
the meaning of Godfather's rhyme belatedly enters my brain: a
trap for a mouse. The only mouse he could mean is Lang.

I hurry past the sugar-coated fruits and out of the orangery.
Godfather already caused the deaths of Lang's brothers with
his clockwork mousetraps. What will he do to Lang? I may have
banished Godfather from this realm, but what has he left behind
for Lang? I must find Lang to warn him of Godfather's trap,

and I must find the nutcracker to warn him of Lang, and I have no idea now where either man is.

In the red and yellow gallery, I look this way and that, spinning in a frantic circle. The blank-eyed faces of the white sugar loaf statues look dully back, offering no clue where I should go. Which way would Lang have gone? Why didn't I bother to ask him what he'd learned before I sent him away?

I force myself into stillness and take a breath. Lang is too clever, too quick, too strong, and too human to fall prey to a mousetrap. I can't worry about him, or even about the nutcracker. It's Clara I should be thinking of.

I look into the next doorway and see a drawing room with walls of silk brocade and gilt furnishings, but no occupants. Everyone has gone to see the confectioner, or at least to see the empty place where the confectioner ought to be. If I'm correct in thinking that it was myself and the nutcracker who dreamt this place into being, then it's no wonder I saw nothing in the gilt and velvet carriage.

How much can I shape this world, I wonder? I remember my certainty that Lang and I would find a side entrance into the castle. When we walked through the alley, we found a door where I expected one to be. Perhaps I could simply will the right passage into being, if I only knew where I wanted to go. Where would young Drosselmeier have hidden himself and Clara?

This is a child's fantasy of what a castle ought to be, full of long halls and high towers. I hardly know what the interior of a real castle should be, either, except from my own childhood picture books. If it were a marzipan and gingerbread castle in the Christmas market, though, I wouldn't expect all of its chambers to connect inside. Only the central tower would be a part of the main structure, while the others would be glued to the interior walls with sugar paste.

Suppose Drosselmeier knows little more than I do about castles. Suppose the central tower is the only true one, and he's gone there with my niece? This is a fairytale world, like Petra's stories, and in the stories the girls are always imprisoned in a tower. I must find the stairs, then, and start climbing.

I go back to the stairway that led Lang and me up to this open gallery. This time, I can see around another corner where the stairs continue upward. Have I created this route by wishing it was there?

I take one last look around the gallery, hoping to see Lang striding up to join me, but he's not here. He won't be looking for me; he'll be looking for the nutcracker. Probably he's already at the top of the tower, while I'm wasting my time down below.

I lift my skirts to avoid tripping myself, and start to climb.

I climb up and up. My legs burn with the effort. I unbuttoned my coat in the warm humid air of the orangery, but now I wish I'd left it behind. The time it would take to remove it seems like an unacceptable delay, so I make do, even as sweat prickles between my shoulder blades and slides down my spine.

Every twenty steps, there is a landing with a narrow window. I'm tempted to pause and catch my breath, but I think of Lang. He wouldn't have stopped. He's a soldier, after all, and must be used to long marches and long rides. The emperor's Grand Army travels tens of miles in a day: what would ten or twenty or thirty minutes of climbing stairs be to Lang? I push myself on.

The physical effort makes it hard to think too much about what I will find at the top, so when I finally reach a landing where there is a door instead of more stairs, I've almost forgotten to be anxious. For a moment, the only thing I feel is relief that I can finally rest my burning legs.

I have just enough presence of mind to imagine very hard that there is no need for locks in this magical castle. When my breath has steadied, I push on the door, and it swings open. I still don't know if I have changed the reality of this place or merely reinforced it, but I am glad not to face a locked door after the long climb.

I push open the door to a circular room hung with tapestries. Lang is not here, but two wide windows let in the light of day, and Clara sits at one of them, looking out. She turns at the sound of the door, and her mouth opens in a perfect little circle. "Aunt Marie!" she says.

Even on my tired legs I would run to her, but the floor is strewn with a sea of pillows. When I step into them, I nearly tread on the nutcracker, who is lying half-buried among them. His scarlet frock coat blends into the red and gold silks and satins that cover the pillows.

He blinks up at me and struggles into a seated position. "Mademoiselle Stahlbaum," he says. "You came."

He holds one arm tight against his ribs, which are bound in bloodied linens. He's not wearing the frock coat; it is merely draped over his bare shoulders. Obviously he is still suffering from his wounds, which makes me feel all the crueler as I say, "I came for Clara."

Clara looks at me from the window seat. She's dressed in a white nightgown, ghostly among the rich colors that decorate the tower room. "Herr Drosselmeier says I'm to be a princess," she says uncertainly.

He nods. "You shall both be princesses," he says. His cheeks are nearly as red as his coat, and his eyes are too bright. "I hoped you would come, Mademoiselle Stahlbaum. I had arranged a grand procession to welcome us—to welcome you—to the capital and escort you to the palace."

That explains the empty carriage Lang and I saw, but perhaps it means I don't control this world after all. Has everything I thought I was influencing here only been coincidence? All the talk of the confectioner, in turn, was perhaps no more than superstition among the creatures that make up the population.

"I saw the procession," I say to the nutcracker. "The carriage was exquisite, and the band was very fine, but I can't stay here. Clara and I must go home." I step carefully around him and pick my way through the pillows to the window seat.

Clara hugs me, but she looks at the nutcracker. "You may stay in my kingdom for as long as you like, Mademoiselle Kaltenborn," he says grandly. "And you, Mademoiselle Stahl-baum. You must stay as well. There's no need to go back out there. My most noble savior—allow me to express my gratitude for all you have done for me, dear lady."

For a moment, I can't even remember what he thinks he's grateful to me for. Then I remember that I have saved him from Lang's wrath, not once, but twice. First during the long-ago Christmas Eve battle, and again during their more recent duel. This time, however, I have led Lang to him, and young Dross-elmeier won't be so thankful when he realizes it.

I look around the circular room. A hundred mice could hide in this confusion of cushions and pillows and rugs, but I don't think Lang would bother to conceal himself if he were here. And if he's not here, then where is he?

The worry about Godfather's trap is a shadow on my heart, but I remind myself of Fritz's confidence that Lang can look after himself. I don't know the extent of his powers, after all. Perhaps he can take on other, even more terrifying forms, espe-cially in this place of magic.

I have to get Clara home, but what of the nutcracker? I did promise Lang that I wouldn't interfere when he confronted young Drosselmeier, but it wouldn't be breaking my word if I can bring the nutcracker away with me and Clara before Lang arrives.

"We have to take care of the prince," Clara whispers sol-emnly in my ear.

"Yes," I say. "Have you been helping Herr Drosselmeier?"

She nods. "He was wounded in battle with a wicked villain."

"Yes, I know of his wounds," I say.

Her round little face is still very serious, and there are dark smudges of sleeplessness under her eyes. Is this the same laughing child who sat in my lap on Christmas Eve? The nutcracker has told her that Lang is a villain, but I can no longer believe that Dietrich Lang is wicked, just as I can no longer believe that young Drosselmeier is an entirely noble and innocent hero.

Clara shouldn't be mixed up in this mess of blood and revenge, and she wouldn't be here if the nutcracker hadn't taken her away from her home and her family, just as he did me so long ago. But at least Clara and I have a family and a home to return to, unlike Lang or the nutcracker.

I look at young Drosselmeier. He has laid back in the pillows again, his eyes closed. What happened to his family? Are his parents still in Nuremberg? Did Godfather's brother ever learn what had happened to his son?

Somehow, given that he lives in our city and not in Nuremberg or the court of Lang's uncle, I doubt that Godfather Drosselmeier has done much to resolve things with the people whose lives he's overturned along the way. And the nutcracker, then, is only doing what was done to him: luring children away from home with the promise that they will be part of a fairy tale. But there is no guarantee that the fairy tale will end happily. Young Drosselmeier didn't marry a princess, and taking me or Clara to act as his princess isn't a true solution either.

Now I'm more sure than ever that I must bring him with us out of this place. "What of your parents, Herr Drosselmeier?" I ask.

He opens his eyes and gives me a look of foggy confusion. "My parents?" he echoes.

"Aren't your father and mother waiting for you in Nuremberg?"

The nutcracker's brow crinkles in confusion. I wait, but he only blinks at me without answering.

"Don't you remember anything of your life before you were cursed?" I press. "I bet your mother is worrying for you, just as Clara's is for her."

He tilts his head to one side, thinking hard. "My mother," he says slowly. "She sews the clothes for Father's puppets."

"Have you seen them since your uncle took you to the palace?" I ask.

"I don't think so," the nutcracker says. He looks worried now, and young—younger than me, though I don't think that can be so. But then, I don't understand the way that time passes in this place.

Clara tugs at my hand. "Is Mama mad at me?" she asks in a small voice.

"No, Schätzchen, of course not!" I say. "She is missing you terribly, and Grandmother is, too. Your papa and Uncle Fritz and everyone have been searching and searching for you. I came here with Lieutenant Lang to find you."

At the mention of Lang's name, however, Clara draws away from me. "Lieutenant Lang is a bad man," she says. "He hurt Herr Drosselmeier."

"Lieutenant Lang was very angry with Herr Drosselmeier," I say, choosing my words carefully. "Because Herr Drosselmeier accidentally hurt his mother. If anyone hurt your mama, you would be upset, wouldn't you?"

Clara nods slowly, but she doesn't step back into my arms.

"You brought that perfidious fiend into my realm?" the nutcracker asks. He sways upright and looks suspiciously around the room.

"He came to help me find Clara," I say. "You should not have taken her away, but we can fix this. Come back with us. You need to see the surgeon, and then we will find your parents again."

"No," he says immediately. "You must stay. You must both stay." His cheeks are still very pink, and his breath comes quickly, as if he is the one who has been climbing the stairs instead of me. "This is my kingdom," he says. He looks at me with bright eyes. "Our kingdom, Mademoiselle Stahlbaum."

He purses his lips, and then, before he can say anything more, there is a soft tearing sound and the ceiling above us disappears.

EIGHTEEN

I LOOK up as Clara screams. A huge figure looms above us. It lifts the roof away, leaving the room where we stand open and exposed to the sky.

"What is that thing?" I ask the nutcracker, though I'm afraid I already know the answer. Every time I've wondered about the dangers of the Kingdom of Dolls, one monster has been at the front of my thoughts.

"The Leckermaul," says the nutcracker, confirming my fear. He sits up again, staring at the hole the monster has left. "The sweet tooth giant."

Is this the trap Godfather spoke of, or is it something I've brought into being with my thoughts? I remember Lang's accusation. If I'm responsible for bringing this creature to the castle with my young niece and the wounded nutcracker, then he must be right, and I do have a cruel imagination.

The giant's body is made of burnt and misshapen twists of pastry. Its lumpy head has wide-set eyes above the line of its mouth, but no nose. Every time it moves, blackened flakes of its body break off, drifting down around us like a mockery of snow. A terrible stench of decay washes over me as it opens a mouth full of teeth like broken walnut shells and stuffs the torn roof of the tower inside.

While I stare in horror, the pale pink marzipan and golden shortbread roof tiles are quickly mashed into a paste that the monster swallows in loud gulps. Soon it will want a second handful. Will it grab for the roof of another tower, or take more of the one where we are? Will it notice if it scoops us up along with the marzipan? Those jagged teeth could crush and tear flesh as well as sweets, and what if it finds it prefers the taste? I don't want to stay and find out.

"We have to get out of the tower," I yell at Clara and the nutcracker.

The nutcracker has been staring upward, just as I have been, but now he clambers to his feet. "Never fear, mademoiselles!" he says as I tug Clara away from the window. The loose frock coat slips from his shoulders and falls to the floor, leaving him bare-chested, except for the bandages around his ribs and shoulder. "I shall steel my knightly courage and face this monster on your behalf. This time, I shall save you."

I've seen his courage, or lack thereof, on the battlefield already. This is no time for empty boasts. "With what?" I ask. "Where are your soldiers? Do you even have a sword?"

His brave face crumples. "I had a sword," he says, looking around. He doesn't have a sword now, not even an empty scabbard belted at his waist. I can't see anything else that seems like it would be useful as a weapon. What does he think he's going to do to defend us? I doubt that throwing pillows at the monster will have much effect.

"Come with us," I say to the nutcracker. "We will find somewhere safer, and then find a way to drive the Leckermaul away, as you did before."

"But we must stay here," he says with puzzled insistence. "We are safe in my castle."

"Not in this tower," I say. "We have to leave."

"No," the nutcracker says. He pushes the door to the stairs

shut. "It's not safe out there."

I stare at him. "The Leckermaul is eating your castle. The Leckermaul is going to eat us, and then we will never see our families again. You'll never see your parents."

He looks back at me, bright flags of color in his cheeks. There is panic in his eyes, I suddenly realize. He is as much of a child as Clara, playing at being a prince in this kingdom. I let go of her and advance on him. "Open the door, Herr Drosselmeier," I say with deliberate softness.

He works his mouth, but no words emerge. I'm considering whether to push him aside when a movement catches my eye. The Leckermaul is reaching for the wall.

I spin back to Clara. Each of the giant's fingers is as big as she is. She scrambles away from its descending hand, but the direction she chooses is also further away from me and from the door.

The Leckermaul pulls at the wall, tearing off a section as wide as a four-poster bed. More bits of burnt pastry float down around us, following a rain of marzipan crumbs. Then, the giant abruptly drops its prize and pulls its hand away with a wordless, moaning roar. The wall folds outward and the floor lurches alarmingly.

I scramble toward Clara. Not until I have a hold of her do I look up and see what has distracted the giant.

A hawk, like the one I saw this morning beside the lake, darts around the Leckermaul's head. With a rumbling growl of annoyance, the monster swats at the bird, but it's like trying to flatten a gnat. The hawk swoops easily away from the blow and returns to dive again at the monster's face.

Clara wraps her arms around my waist and buries her face in my coat. "I want to go home," she says.

I put a hand on her tangled hair and look around. With half the wall gone, I can see down into the plaza before the castle. The crowd that had come to meet the confectioner has scattered. The gilded carriage, still empty, stands abandoned before the steps of the main entrance. The nutcracker's soldiers, I note sourly, display as much courage as their prince, for there is no sign of any armed force to defend the castle from the Leckermaul.

The hawk dives at the giant's head again, and again the giant swings at it. This time the blow goes wide and, while it misses the hawk, it strikes one of the adjoining towers. The hollow marzipan walls crumple and fold like wet paper. I hope my earlier theory is correct and the other towers are empty, for anyone inside must be badly injured in the destruction.

The Leckermaul is properly angry now, growling and yawping and flailing its blackened arms around. Two more towers go down as the hawk harries the huge creature. Then the hawk dives behind the giant, so quickly that the Leckermaul loses sight of it and stands casting about blindly. I'm searching the sky, too, when I spot the dark shape careening down toward us.

With a heavy ruffling of wing feathers, the hawk breaks its dive just before it hits our tower. The air shivers around its form, and then it is Dietrich Lang who lands hard among the pillows on the floor of the tower room. My heart lifts, for he is whole and unharmed. He hasn't been caught in any of Godfather's traps.

Lang stands up, chest heaving for breath.

"Fiend!" the nutcracker cries.

Lang ignores him, looking at me instead. "You have the child," he says. "Take her out of here."

"Come with me," I say. "We'll all go. We'll find a way to resolve this."

Lang glances to the nutcracker, then turns back to me. "Marie," he says fiercely. "No discussion. Go."

"What are you going to do to him?" I ask. "He is already miserable and broken."

Behind Lang, the nutcracker's face has gone from a feverish

flush to bloodless gray. He doesn't move toward us, but seems frozen in place.

"You took an oath," Lang says, his voice rising. "You swore not to stand in my way when I found him."

"I am not standing in your way," I return. "But he was a child when Godfather took him from his family, and he's been trapped ever since. Look at him—what can you do that is worse than what he already suffers?"

"I'm not going to argue with you," Lang says. He doesn't look at the nutcracker. Instead, he points to where the Leckermaul is still looking for the hawk. "You can't stay here."

"You took an oath, too," I remind him. "We must bring Clara safely home. I'm not leaving without you."

Clara, hearing her name, chooses this moment to lift her face. When she sees Lang, she squeaks in alarm and tries to run away. The scattered pillows catch her feet. She trips and falls to the floor, a short length from the open drop where the giant pulled the wall away.

"Clara!" I cry. "Don't move!"

She sits up and wails.

The sound catches the Leckermaul's attention. It turns back toward us, abandoning its fruitless search, and reaches toward our tower again. It will peel away more of the wall, the floor will collapse, and we will all fall to our deaths.

But the nutcracker finally unfreezes. He runs toward the giant's descending hand. I don't know what he's going to do exactly, but it must be something foolish and uselessly heroic. "No!" I cry, but before I can try to stop him, Lang grabs my arm and pulls me back.

The nutcracker leaps upward and throws himself onto one of the giant's fingers, wrapping his arms and legs around it.

The Leckermaul lifts its hand and peers at this new annoyance. Its eyes are a shining collection of baked currants, like the segmented eyes of a fly. Does it see one nutcracker, or a repeated kaleidoscope image of him? Either way, it shakes its hand, trying to dislodge him. If it does, he will go flying and nothing good will happen when he lands. If we die in this dream world, will we wake at home, or is that the end?

Then the floor shifts beneath my feet, and I can't spare any more attention for wondering about Herr Drosselmeier's fate. After the giant's pawing, this tower is crumpling like the others.

I look over and see the carpet, with Clara on top of it, sliding slowly toward the open edge of the tower. A crimson pillow next to her tumbles off and disappears from view.

"Get the child," Lang says. He kneels and grabs hold of the edge of the carpet, stopping its movement.

"Hold on, Schätzchen," I call to Clara as I begin to pick my way through the pillows toward her. The furnishings that made the room seem cozy when I first entered now feel treacherous, ready to slip from under my feet at any moment. I get down on my hands and knees, crawl toward her, and stretch out my hand.

She turns her tear-streaked face to me and slowly begins to crawl away from the edge. It seems an age before she's finally close enough that I can catch her hand and pull her into my arms. I get her into my lap and scoot carefully away from the drop until the door is at my back.

The giant is sitting down on the plaza, looking at its hand, which is now missing a finger. I can't read enough of its features to tell if it is pained or puzzled, but at least it isn't pulling the rest of the castle apart right now.

I look at Lang. He's still kneeling beside the carpet, and he meets my gaze grimly. "Try the door," he says.

Should I ask if he saw what happened to the nutcracker? I don't want Clara to hear the answer. I don't know if *I* want to hear the answer.

I turn and push at the door. It doesn't move. The frame is bent around it. The tower is still sagging. The movement is slow, but inevitable.

"The stairs probably aren't safe anyway," Lang says. "The whole thing may collapse." He moves closer and sits beside me, tilting his head back against the remaining solid wall with a sigh.

"Will you fly away?" I ask.

He turns his head to me. There are new lines around his eyes and mouth since we parted in the orangery, all of them speaking of exhaustion and none of humor. "No," he says shortly. "I will not."

"I think we must wake up to leave," I say. "My godfather was here, but I made him yawn, and he disappeared."

"I'm not finished here," Lang says. He doesn't leap up to go after the nutcracker, however.

"Herr Drosselmeier is gone," I say. I can't say it to Lang, but I hope the nutcracker took my reminder about his parents to heart. Maybe he has woken himself and is home in Nuremberg. Maybe he is even now reuniting with the parents who have gone so long without their son.

In my lap, Clara sniffles and wipes her nose. "I want to go home now," she says.

"We'll go soon," I say. "This dream has gone sour. It's time to wake up."

"You don't know what happens when you wake," Lang counters.

"Last time, I woke in my own bed with my mother scolding me for oversleeping," I say. "That sounds quite pleasant compared to our current situation." I hold Clara with one arm and reach out to Lang with my other hand.

Just thinking about waking, I feel a subtle pressure in my ears, the first sensation of the building yawn. I let it come, opening my mouth just as Clara does the same.

Lang shakes his head. I can see the muscles tighten along his jaw, even as the remaining castle towers beyond him waver. He's fighting it. "Dietrich," I say around another yawn. "Come with me. It's time to wake."

His features twitch, but he still doesn't take my hand. Instead, I grab hold of his wrist. "No," he says, but the word turns into a yawn.

I twine our fingers together. The dream world is dissolving around us. I yawn so wide that my eyes water. When I open them again, I see great billows of fog rising from the lake beyond the castle.

And then, we fall through the sky.

NINETEEN

W E FALL through silver clouds, full of frost and spun sugar. I hold tight to my companions. The hard edges of Lang's crowns cut into my fingers, but I can't let go of him or Clara.

What if we drift apart as we float down through this thick mist? I hoped I would wake in my bed, but now I don't know where we will come to rest; I only know that I don't want to lose either of them.

I think I see shapes in the fog: glittering feathers of frost, or perhaps white swan's down. Far off and obscured by the clouds, I glimpse something shaped like a man. Is it the nutcracker, returning to the waking world somewhere alongside us? I can't make out the person's face and suddenly I remember the poor featureless sailor-figures who went down with the brass ship in the lake. Perhaps they felt as I do now, sinking into something I can't see.

Am I drowning in this fog? I open my mouth to speak or breathe or scream or simply call out into the void, but then we land with a soft whoosh. The fog becomes a bright white cloud that wraps around me in a shiver of sound and cold.

Clara slips out of my grasp.

"Clara!" I cry. "Clara!" I can't lose her again, after all I've done to find her. I sit up and realize that we are in a winter forest of leafless beeches. The snow is deep and powdery, and we sank into it when we landed from… from whatever we passed through between here and the Kingdom of Dolls. I scrabble through the powder and pull Clara out.

She shivers and clutches at me. "Aunt Marie," she says, "I want to go home."

"I know, Schätzchen," I say. "So do I." I try to brush the snow from her night gown before it melts, then pick her up in my arms. My shoulder is still not quite right, but I can ignore it for a while. Just until we find somewhere warm for Clara. I'm glad now that I never took off my coat, but I am definitely missing my mittens. Clara doesn't even have stockings on—she can't stay out here in the snow.

"Is Lieutenant Lang gone now?" she asks.

"No, he came with us," I say. I look around. Lang will know what to do—but where I expect to see him, there is only another crater in the powdery snow.

I shift Clara onto my hip and paw through the snow with my free hand until I catch hold of his arm. "Lieutenant Lang! Get up!" I haul on his arm, lose my balance, and sprawl awkwardly in the snow with Clara.

She whimpers and shivers. "C-cold."

"I know, Schätzchen, I'm sorry."

I give her the slippers I've been carrying in my pocket, then struggle out of my coat, wrap her in it, and return to Lang. I find his arm again and brush the snow away until I clear his face. His eyes are closed, and his skin is pale.

"Lang!" I say, shaking his shoulders. "Dietrich!"

He doesn't respond, and gnawing unease blooms in my belly. I pull him into a more upright position and place my hand against his neck, hoping to feel the beat of his heart. I think perhaps he's a little warmer under his collar, but I can't find his pulse.

"Is he dead?" Clara asks in a tiny, frightened voice.

"No," I say. "Of course not." My fingers are numb from the snow, that's why I can't feel his heartbeat. That must be why.

I work my hands under his armpits, around his torso, and heave with all my might. This moves him out of the loose snow and onto the more packed spot where Clara and I have been thrashing around, but he is still as animate and cooperative as a sack of grain.

He's not dead. He can't be. He's far too vital to have been killed by a soft landing in a snowdrift.

I sit back on my heels in the snow and the unknown forest and swallow hard against the tightness in my chest and the tears pricking in my eyes. He held the brass ship above the water by force of will, carried me through icy water, and distracted the giant that would have killed us without even knowing what it did. He defeated the nutcracker in their duel without breaking a sweat. He must be alive. I can't consider any other possibility.

"Aunt Marie?" Clara says.

"I'm going to get us home, Clärchen," I tell her. "Don't worry."

The cold is creeping through my dress, but I can't take my coat from Clara, who has even less to protect her than I. I look around, wishing for a grove of pine trees where we could shelter under the boughs, but all I can see is white snow and the dark trunks of the beeches.

I maneuver Lang so his head is in my lap, and put my cold fingers beneath his collar again. I still can't find his pulse, but he must have one. I unwork the frogs of his attila and slide my hand over his chest beneath the jacket. For a moment, I close my eyes and concentrate on what I can feel with my palm over his heart.

Finally, I feel the soft thump of his heartbeat. Relief floods through me, and I have to swallow down sudden tears.

"He's alive!" I tell Clara, but she only blinks at me.

I start to close up his jacket, then I notice something inside his collar: a small silver whistle. It's held on a slender silver chain around his neck. I find the clasp and unhook it, then lift the whistle and blow. It makes a high, thin sound. I shake it and blow again, but my second attempt is no louder than the first. When I thread the chain around Lang's neck, though, I see his lids move, as if he's looking for something without opening his eyes.

"Dietrich." I pat his cheek and smooth the hair from his cold forehead. "Wake up."

His eyes flicker again, but only briefly. I hook the clasp, tuck the whistle beneath his attila, and close the frogs.

Around us, the forest is shading into gray. Night is coming, and that means it will only grow colder.

"Dietrich," I try again. "You have to wake up." I need to get Clara out of the snow, but I can't leave him like this, and I can't carry both of them. Now I wish he were a mouse, for then I could put him in my pocket, pick Clara up, and start walking.

Clara has pulled my coat up around her ears. I can't see her face, only a miserable huddle of dark wool. My ears and fingers are numb, and even in my boots, my feet aren't much better off.

This isn't how things are supposed to go—to find Clara and escape from the Kingdom of Dolls, only to freeze to death in the snow? No, I can't let this be the end.

I smack Lang's chest with the flat of my hand. "Wake up! Or I will leave you here to die. Wake! Up!" I smack him again and again, using the blows to punctuate my words. Clara peeks out at me, looking alarmed.

Then, finally, he shifts his head on my lap. His hand comes up, and he swats weakly at me. I catch his hand in mine and pull his fingers to my lips, kissing them. "Get up before you freeze to death," I tell him.

He blinks at me, but he struggles into a sitting position and looks around. "Where are we?" he asks.

"I don't know," I say. "Put your pelisse on all the way. It's cold."

He nods and slowly undoes the cord which holds the pelisse over his shoulders. Then his eyes focus on me. "Where is your coat?"

"Clara needed it."

He looks at the woolen lump where Clara is hiding her face again, and holds the fur-lined pelisse out to me. I hesitate, because he was comatose only a minute ago, but then I take it, because I am cold and he still has his attila jacket.

I shake the snow from the garment and shrug my arms into the sleeves. "Can you stand up?" I ask Lang. "We have to find somewhere out of the snow."

He nods, but when he stands, he sways. I reach out to steady him, and he frowns at me. "I have overextended," he says.

I remember his hands, white-knuckled on the rail of the brass ship. "I can keep us afloat," he'd said, "but there's a cost." All the magic he used to keep us alive in the Kingdom of Dolls—there was a price, and he is paying it now.

I pick Clara up and settle her on one hip. On my other side, I wrap my arm around Lang. Before we can begin a slow shuffle through the deep snow, however, I hear a distant jingle echoing through the bare trees.

Lang looks at me, then into the darkening forest. He pulls himself upright, unsheathes his saber, and steps out to meet whoever—whatever—is approaching us.

The jingle sounds closer. Clara clutches herself tight against me, and I brace my legs in the snow. Should we run? Can I run through the snow while carrying Clara? I'll find a way to do it if I must.

But what appears between the trees is a riderless horse. Lang sags from his guard stance to lean on his saber as if it is a crutch. With his other hand, he fumbles into his attila, pulls out the silver whistle, and blows two short blasts on it.

The horse pricks its ears and steps up its pace, though the snow is deep enough that it is having trouble making forward progress. It's a large bay with a white face: the horse Lang rode away on after the duel.

It stops in front of him and pushes his chest with its head. Lang grabs the bridle to steady himself, then rubs the animal's nose, speaking softly to it. After a moment, the tall stallion lowers its front legs to kneel in the snow, and Lang turns to me.

"Come," he says. "Kuno will carry us all."

I flounder through the snow to the horse. Lang helps me into the saddle, and I cradle Clara against me. She's only half-awake, slipping away into the false safety of sleep. I chafe her arms through the coat. "We're going home, Schätzchen," I tell her, but she doesn't reply.

Lang mounts behind me, then there is a tenuous moment while the stallion—Kuno—struggles back to its feet in the snow. Finally, the horse is standing again, and it begins to walk through the trees. Lang puts his arms around me, and I'm glad we can share what little body warmth we have left.

The horse makes its slow way through the snowy forest as the light leaches away. Everything is shadows by the time I make out a gap in the trees. There must be a path, or even a road, up ahead.

Lang has gone slack behind me. I think he must have lapsed back into unconsciousness. I clamp my elbows over his arms as the horse struggles out of the deep snow and onto a road of frozen mud, churned and rutted by passing wagons. I don't know which way to go, but Kuno turns left without pausing.

We've only been on the road for a few minutes when I hear new hoof beats approaching ahead. Friend or foe? Surely any fellow traveler must take pity and help us on this bitter winter night. I can't see in the dark, but the stallion twitches its ears forward with interest. That must be a good sign. I hope it is.

The other rider is almost on top of us when he calls out,

"Who goes there?" and I nearly topple all three of us off the horse with surprise and relief. Never in my life have I been so glad to hear my brother's voice.

"Fritz!" His name comes out as a croak, and I have to try again. "Fritz, it's me."

"Good God," Fritz says. "Marie? Is Lang with you?"

"Yes," I say. "And we have Clara."

"Where was she? No, never mind, you'll tell me later." He moves his horse closer, and I lift the folds of the coat to show Clara in my arms. She blinks at him and burrows closer to me.

Fritz swears under his breath and looks at the slumped form of Lang behind me. "What happened to Lang? Is he wounded?"

"He's not well," I say. I can't even begin to explain right now. "We need to get out of the snow. Where are we?"

"The wood beyond the eastern gate," Fritz says.

It's a relief to hear that we're not so far from home after all, but we still need to get out of the cold. "Take Clärchen," I say to Fritz.

He shakes his head. "No, you must stay with her." He makes Fox sidestep close to Kuno, who stands still as a statue. "I'll take Lang."

My first instinct is to refuse. I know Clara will be safe with Fritz, but I don't want to be separated from Lang. True to his oath, he protected me throughout our journey in the Kingdom of Dolls, and now I want to protect him in turn. I need to keep him close, to hold on to him, to feel the slight movement against my back that lets me know he's still breathing.

I know what my brother is thinking, though. I'm already riding astride with my skirts up around my knees. What will people say when we return to the city and I'm on a horse with the very man who was challenged to a duel over my honor?

I find I care very little for propriety at the moment. Gossip can't frighten me after all the other challenges I have faced. On the other hand, if Fritz cares, he's entirely capable of being stubborn about it. An argument with my brother will be a further delay when Clara and Lang need to be taken to shelter as quickly as possible. "Very well," I say.

Lang is a dead weight at my back, but somehow Fritz hauls him across from one horse to the other. Perhaps it's something he's done often as a soldier: carrying wounded men out of danger.

Lang isn't wounded, I remind myself. Only overextended. That means he'll recover. He must.

I tighten my arms around Clara, touch my heels to Kuno's sides, and we move through the forest, toward home.

TWENTY

"WHAT day is it?" I ask Fritz.

"The twenty-seventh of December," he replies. "Just as it was this morning. Where did you go? How did you end up in the forest?"

"You first," I say. If it's the same day, then only a few hours have passed here during all that long night and day in the Kingdom of Dolls. "I think your story will be shorter. Why were you riding through the forest? I'm glad that you were, but why didn't you wait at Godfather's workshop?"

"You and Lang both disappeared," he says. "I looked everywhere in the workshop, and you were gone. So I thought, what's the point of staying here, where I can't do anything useful? I was going to take Kuno back to the barracks when he went off like a mad thing."

My dear, practical brother. Apparently, I'm not the only one who can't simply sit still and wait. "I'm glad that you were able to follow him," I say. "I didn't know where we were, or what I was going to do with both Lang and Clara."

I peek into the folds of my coat at Clara. Her eyes are closed, and she looks nearly as bad as Lang. "We're going home, Schätzchen," I whisper to her. "We'll be home soon." She doesn't reply, and I wrap the coat more tightly around her.

"Where did you go?" Fritz asks again. "Did you—did you really go to another world, Marie? If I hadn't seen you—"

"We did," I say. "Godfather was there, and his nephew. It is all as I told you before, and as Lang told you in the workshop."

He shakes his head, then moves to steady Lang's inert body. "If I hadn't seen you," he repeats. "The Kingdom of Dolls?"

"Yes." It's all I can say. I'm so tired and I've told him the story so many times before. If he's decided to believe it now, I'm glad—but he could have believed me the first time and saved everyone a good deal of trouble and heartache. "I'll tell you everything that happened, only let us get somewhere warm first."

"I will listen," he says, and there is an unusual earnestness in his voice that makes my eyes suddenly prick with tears. I blink them away.

We emerge from the trees, and I see the orange light of the torches along the city walls. We are crossing the same snow field where Lang and Drosselmeier began their duel at dawn. I can hardly make myself think of it as yesterday morning. It feels like a month or a year ago. So much has happened since I left home that morning.

I feel as weary as Lang. Perhaps it is an aftereffect of having lived a day in the span of an hour. If I didn't have to focus on holding onto Clara and staying upright on the horse, I might pass out, too. But we are almost home. Almost.

We approach the city walls. They loom reassuringly above me. There are no giants here, and the walls are made of solid things like earth and stone. Nothing can tear them down so easily as the Leckermaul ripped apart the nutcracker's castle.

The gate hasn't yet been barred for the night. We enter beneath the curious gazes of the watchmen and start through the streets. As with the walls, every ordinary citizen I see is a reminder that I am home again. Soon we will reach my parents' house, and then what will I do? Even if my brother has come around to a tenuous belief in magic, that doesn't mean anyone else in my family will have changed their minds.

"What will we say?" I ask Fritz. "You know I can't tell Father and Mother where we've been."

"Best to keep it simple," he says. "Tell them as much of the truth as they will believe. Leave things out, but don't make up anything you'll have to remember later."

Simple. I can do that. "I remembered a place where I hid as a child, and thought Clara might be there," I say. "I went after her, and Lieutenant Lang happened to be nearby in his search for Herr Drosselmeier. I found Clara, Lang abandoned his search to help us, and then you found all of us."

"That sounds well enough," Fritz says. "But didn't you find Herr Drosselmeier there? In that other place?"

I think of the nutcracker leaping at the Leckermaul's huge hand. What happened to him? That's a question that will remain unanswered unless I return to the Kingdom of Dolls, and right now, I only want to go home. "We found him," I say, "and lost him again."

We turn up the lane toward our house, passing between the familiar shapes of our neighbors' homes. There are the Doerffers' clean-swept stairs. There are the dead stalks in the flower boxes in front of the Leszinskis' house. I know the shape of every wall and window of these houses.

A man comes running down to meet us. It is Johann. Some-one must have noticed us and run ahead of the doubly laden horses' walking pace with the news of our coming.

"Do you have her?" he asks breathlessly.

I start to hand Clärchen down to him. She clutches at me, whimpering, until I say, "Schätzchen, it's your papa. We're home now. We're safe." Then she tumbles down into her father's arms and begins to cry, great hiccupping wails that echo off the walls of the houses. She's loud enough that even Lang stirs briefly. All the neighbors will know that she's been found.

Johann carries Clara away, and I huddle forward in the unfamiliar saddle. A winter wind scuttles down the lane, blowing into my face and over my legs where my skirts are drawn up. The cold was bearable when I had Lang at my back and Clara bundled before me, but now I feel entirely exposed. I trade my hands back and forth, one on the reins and the other within the fur-lined sleeve of Lang's pelisse as we cover the final distance to the house.

My father is the next to meet us as we walk the weary horses into the yard. He helps Fritz carry Lang indoors and to the spare bedchamber. I trail behind, letting my brother do the explaining. His military training is obvious as he reports quickly and succinctly to my father, giving a very truthful-sounding story of how we all came to be in the winter woods. When my mother hurries into the room, he repeats it for her, too.

"Marie," my mother scolds. "You shouldn't have gone off by yourself." Then she bursts into tears and wraps her arms around me. "But if you hadn't gone," she sobs, "who knows what would have happened? Oh, my darling, you are so brave and so foolish!"

I'm too tired to cry with her, but I lean into her embrace. At the same time, her warmth around me reminds me of all that Lang doesn't have. "I couldn't have brought her back without Lieutenant Lang's help," I say. "He protected us both."

She finds her handkerchief and wipes her eyes, then looks at Lang, who is lying white and motionless atop the coverlet of the bed. My father has built up the fire, but the warmth hasn't had any effect on Lang yet.

"We'll do everything we can for him, then," she says. "Herr Wendelstern is tending to Clara, then he'll look in on the lieutenant."

I want to stay with Lang and wait for the surgeon's opinion, but my mother draws me away upstairs. My fingers feel swollen and hot now that I'm inside. I remember that I've worn the same dress through lakes and snowbanks and it is in as sorry a state as I am.

"I want a bath," I tell my mother.

"Of course," she says. "And some hot soup." She goes to tell Dora to heat the water, and I sit down at my dressing table. My face in the mirror is red-cheeked as warmth returns to my body, but my eyes are shadowed. I put my fingers to my bare collarbone. The golden chain of my necklace is in my coat pocket, and the coat is with Clara. If it didn't fall out somewhere in the snow, then I will clasp it around my neck again, but I will no longer have the seven circlets to string on it. The urge to reach for them will fade with time, surely.

My mother returns with a tray. There is not only soup, but bread and cheese and sausage. As soon as I see it, I realize how ravenously hungry I am. It's still too confusing for my mind to decide if the time within the dream world was a day or an hour, but the timekeeper within my stomach is quite clear: it has been far too long since I ate.

"Lieutenant Lang has had a great shock from the cold," my mother tells me as I start in on the food. "The same as poor Clärchen. I can't imagine how you are still standing upright, Mariechen. As soon as you've had your bath, you must go straight to bed." She hugs me again, as if she needs to verify that I am really here. When she pulls back, she looks puzzled. "You smell of rose water," she says.

"Do I?" I ask. I sniff a few times. The scent has been so ever-present that I stopped noticing it long ago. "My nose is all stuffed up from the cold."

She looks at my dressing table and the few stoppered bottles I have there. "Perhaps you spilled some."

"Yes," I say. "That could have happened." It's a more believable explanation than saying that I nearly drowned in a lake of it, and she seems to accept it.

"Straight to bed," she says again.

150

Dora brings up the hot water and clucks over me, and then, finally, they both leave and I'm alone. I strip away my layers of clothing and step into the bath. It's so hot it stings my skin. I sink into it gratefully, welcoming the sharpness of the sensation it brings.

I scrub until I'm sure that I've removed all traces of the rose water lake from myself, then lay back in the cooling water. My mind swirls with all that has occurred since Christmas Eve. Everything I waited so long for has happened: the nutcracker came for me, and I returned to the Kingdom of Dolls. I even found a way for my brother to believe the truth of my adventures. And yet, nothing is as I expected it to be. Instead, everything is topsy-turvy and upside down.

My eyes grow heavy as I try to make sense of it all. I nearly slip below the surface of the bathwater, then start awake and laugh darkly at myself. After all the trouble to avoid drowning in the dream world, I can't let myself fall asleep in the bath. The water has cooled anyway. I climb out carefully, put on my nightgown, and crawl into bed just as my mother comes back to check on me.

She smooths my damp hair back and kisses my forehead. "We will all feel better in the morning, after a good night's sleep," she tells me. "This day has overwrought us all."

I yawn out some kind of reply and close my eyes, falling straight into a sleep as thick and enveloping as treacle. In my dreams, the clockwork ship sinks while I stand on the deck, as helpless as the carved wooden sailors. The Leckermaul's giant hands reach for me in the castle tower and I'm frozen, watching them come. I can't move and when I finally manage to leap away at the last moment, I fall and fall and fall.

I sit up in bed, cold sweat coating my body. All is quiet and dark. I'm in my own familiar room, with the lamps and the wallpaper and the furnishings that have all been here as long as I can remember. There is even the same little table beside the bed where the mouse king once climbed up to demand my sugar-plums.

Suddenly, I need to see Dietrich Lang. I need to know that he is real, that I am real, that all of what has happened to us together is real.

I pull on my dressing gown, creep down the stairs, and quietly let myself into the spare bedchamber.

Twenty-One

I SHUT tthe door and press my back to it as I look around
the room. A lamp burns on the table, casting its glow against
the warm shadows from the coal grate. Lang is a still form
beneath the coverlet. In the chair beside the bed, Maunzi yawns,
stretches, and curls into a circle to resume his nap.

The cat, sleeping beside the former mouse king. The very
thought of it is so ridiculous that it can't help but push away
some of the strange, helpless terror of my dreams. Does Maunzi
know what Lang once was? Could Lang speak to the cat, the way
he spoke to the swans in the Kingdom of Dolls?

I approach the bed and look down at Lang. His uniform
has been removed. From what I can see above the coverlet,
he's wearing a simple linen shirt. Below the bedclothes—well, I
shouldn't speculate about that. Instead, I look at his face, where
a day's growth of beard darkens his cheeks. The image of him
standing tall in his uniform, his lips quirked into a wry smile, is
so strong in my mind. It is strange to see him like this, prone
and still.

Even in sleep, though, he doesn't appear entirely relaxed. A
line of worry remains on his forehead, and there is a tightness
around his mouth.

I want to stroke his forehead or hold his hand, but I don't want to wake him. After all our adventures, after all his exertions, he needs the sleep. I suppose I need the sleep, too, but I don't want to go back to my bed. I still want to be close to him, though I'm not sure if it's because I want his protection or because I want to protect him.

When I look at his mouth, I remember the kiss we shared and my thoughts before it. His touch has left its imprint upon me, after all. Have I, though, left a similar imprint upon him?

I scoop Maunzi out of the chair and sit, tucking my feet up beneath me. How long will Lang sleep? A day? A week? And when he wakes, what look will he give me? Maybe he will be angry with me for taking him out of the Kingdom of Dolls before he could complete his revenge on the nutcracker.

But he wasn't angry in the snowy forest. He was still doing his best to protect me and Clara, standing between us and potential danger, even though he could barely stand at all. The thought brings a surge of warm, tender feeling in my heart. I start to reach for him, but at the same moment, Maunzi stretches up to tap my leg with his paws.

I look down at the cat, who jumps into my lap. He settles himself as he wishes and begins to purr, clearly indicating that it is time for me to sit quietly. That's probably the best course of action. Morning will come, Lang will open his eyes, and we'll see what happens then. I settle back in the chair and close my eyes, listening to Maunzi's purring, Lang's breathing, and the small noises of the fire.

All is still and perfectly mundane after the fantastical events of the last days. Maunzi is a warm weight anchoring me in this room, this night, this world.

When the clock on the mantel chimes and brings me back to wakefulness, the deepest hours of the night have passed. The room has cooled as winter pushes in on us again. I set Maunzi down and kneel on the hearth to add coal to the fire.

I watch the flames lick around the new lumps until I become aware that I, too, am being watched. When I turn, I see the soft gleam of the flames reflected in Lang's open eyes.

"Marie," he says softly.

I go to the bed, where I can look into his face in the low light. He blinks up at me. There's still that line between his brows, the one I want to wipe away with my fingers. I hesitate a moment, then sit on the edge of the bed. "We are in my family's house," I say, assuming that will answer his first questions.

He takes this in, but the concern doesn't disappear from his face. "The child, too?" he asks.

"She's with her parents," I assure him. "We brought her home safely."

"You brought her home," he says.

"Only with your assistance." I want to take his hand in mine, but even in this close darkness, I hesitate to close the distance between us. "You are safe here, too," I add. "For as long as you need to recover."

Lang gives me a long look, then turns his face away, into the shadows. "Why?" he asks. "Why do you take me in? You know what I am."

A man, a mouse, a hawk—Dietrich Lang is many things, and it will be a long time before I can resolve him into one image. "You saved my life," I say. "Several times over. I could no more have left you in the snow than I could have left Clara."

"You have seen me," he presses. "You know I might become a beast in the blink of an eye."

"But you are a man," I say. "You could have remained an animal for all your days, but you chose to be a man. And you chose to save me. In the tower, you could simply have drawn on the nutcracker, but instead you took the time to tell me to run."

He is silent for a long time. The coals settle on the grate with a soft sound. Maunzi sits up on the chair and begins to wash his face. Finally, Lang speaks again.

"I took an oath to protect you," he says. He turns to meet my eyes again, his face still painted with shadows in the firelight. "I didn't want to fail you, the way I failed her." The words tumble out, gaining power as he speaks. "I couldn't save my mother, but I could save you—"

He stops suddenly and turns his face away again. His whole body quivers, and his breath grows ragged. I have a moment of panic, thinking that something terrible is happening to his fatigued body. Then I realize that he is weeping.

I find his hand in the bedclothes and link our fingers together. He holds on to me as tightly as if we were falling again, with no knowledge of when and where we might land.

I don't say anything, for what can I say? His mother—in Godfather's story, the nutcracker was to take seven steps backward to end the curse on the princess. But the mouse queen threw herself beneath his feet on the seventh step. Young Drosselmeier broke her back, thus transferring the curse to himself. Now that I'm thinking of choices, I can see that Lang's mother, too, had a choice. She had one living child left, and yet she still chose death and revenge for the husband and children who had already been killed. Lang was there. He watched her make that choice, and she didn't choose him.

Lang tugs at our joined hands. I lie down close beside him, unlinking our fingers and wrapping my arms around him instead. I wish I could hold all his broken pieces together and make him whole again. Like young Drosselmeier, he was a child thrown into a terrifying situation he could not change. Where the nutcracker retreated into the Kingdom of Dolls, though, Dietrich Lang went out into the world looking to right the wrongs he had seen.

Gradually, Lang's tears ebb away. The clock strikes again. We've passed through the night and are coming to the morning. I should go back to my own bed before anyone finds me here, but I don't want to leave him.

"You are safe," I say. "And I am safe."

"For the moment," he says, and there is a hint of his old wry humor in the words. He puts his arm around me and exhales, a release of long held tension. "I hope it will be a long moment."

"So do I," I say. I want to keep him here in the warm darkness until his heart can heal from all its hurts, but all I can do is press myself closer against him. I stroke his rough, wet cheeks and run my fingers through his hair. Gradually, he returns the touches, sliding his hand over my arm and shoulder, smoothing my hair. I feel him press a kiss to the top of my head, then he catches my hand and kisses my knuckles, too.

I lift my face to his, and we kiss with salt-tinged lips. One kiss becomes another, then becomes a dozen small explorations of lips on lips, lips on cheeks and eyelids and earlobes.

"Marie," he says. "I've seen many curses, but I think you may be the first blessing I've known."

I pillow my head on his shoulder and lay my palm flat on his chest, over his heart and the scar he bears, where I can feel the even rise and fall of his breaths. Sleep carries us away, and I don't wake until I hear the door to the bedchamber open.

Lang's arms are still around me, but the small sounds that woke me haven't yet woken him. I carefully shift myself out of his embrace and sit up with my heart in my throat. Maunzi, who had been curled up near our feet, jumps down. I'm lying atop the bedclothes in my dressing gown, but that's not much to balance against being discovered here with him, rather than in my own bed.

The faint gray light of morning shows my brother in the doorway, his face tight and severe.

"Fritz," I begin. "I can explain." I don't get farther than that, though, because I don't actually know how I'm going to explain any of this. I have been fully clothed all night, but what passed between Lang and me was every bit as intimate as my brother must assume on finding us twined together. Beside me, Lang stirs and unhelpfully puts his arm around my waist again.

Fritz's mouth thins. "Marie," he says in a low hiss through his teeth. He steps into the room and closes the door, though not before Maunzi makes an exit.

Lang sits up slowly. I feel the heat of his presence at my back, and I'm immensely relieved that he is once again warm and moving.

My brother, however, looks considerably less approving. "Marie," he says again. "You have one minute to leave this room."

I open my mouth to argue, but Lang takes his arm from around me. "Go," he says softly into my ear. "It will be all right."

"Marie," my brother grinds out a third time, but I have absolutely no intention of leaving these two alone together. If they want to argue or fight about me, they can do it in front of me.

"What are you going to do, Fritz?" I ask. "Challenge him to a duel? He could hardly stand up last night, and even if he were well, I saw him fight with Drosselmeier, and I won't let the same happen to you."

"You insult me if you think I wouldn't acquit myself better than that puppet," Fritz says stiffly.

"You insult me if you think I'm going to sit idly by and let either of you hurt the other," I return.

"There is no need for insults," Lang says from behind me. "I know you are both too stubborn to avoid an argument, but let me save you the trouble. I won't take up arms against you, Stahlbaum. Not today, for every muscle in my body hurts, and I couldn't lift a blade if I wanted to. Not on any other day, either. I have lost all of my own brothers—do you really think I would take Marie's from her?"

TWENTY-TWO

"SIT down, Stahlbaum," Lang says to Fritz, pointing at the chair by the bed.

Fritz only glares at both of us.

"You don't even know what happened between when we left Godfather's workshop and when you found us in the forest," I point out. "Please, at least listen. You said you would."

Reluctantly, my brother sits down. Yesterday, when he found us unexpectedly in the forest, he seemed ready to believe in the magic I've experienced. I hope he can set aside his concerns about my honor long enough to listen to us now.

"You disappeared from the workshop," he prompts. "With the clockwork ship."

"We were transported to the middle of a lake of rose water," I say, and, bit by bit, Lang and I tell him everything that occurred in the Kingdom of Dolls. Almost everything—neither of us mentions our kiss outside the marzipan castle. I keep my seat on the bed beside Lang, though, and while my brother may be stubborn, he's not stupid. As he takes in the details of our adventure, however, he seems to forget his objections about my being here with Lang and focus on the problem at hand.

"Is he dead, then? Young Drosselmeier?" he asks.

"I don't know," I say. Beside me, Lang frowns, but says nothing. "He disappeared. I can only hope that he returned to Nuremberg and his parents."

"And what of Godfather?" Fritz says.

"Did you go back to the clockmaker's workshop?" Lang asks. "There might be some sign of him there."

Fritz shakes his head. "I didn't go back. I followed Kuno, found you, brought you both home. By the time the surgeon left, I had forgotten all about Godfather."

"We must look for him, then," Lang says grimly.

"First, we should look here," I say. "Is the nutcracker still in the toy cabinet? That will give us some clue."

We all exchange looks, then Fritz stands. "Let's check," he says.

I get to my feet as well, but Lang hesitates.

My brother looks at him. "Are you honestly so weakened, Lang? You're not just playing it up to avoid a fight?"

"Yes," Lang says. "The magic takes a good deal out of me. I do not use it lightly. And flying uses different muscles than what is required to ride a horse." He shrugs demonstratively, then grimaces.

"What's the point of magic if it leaves you flat on your back after?" my brother asks. He sighs dramatically. "Very well."

He shoos me out of the room. This time I go, leaving Fritz to help Lang out of bed and into a dressing gown while I wait in the hall. Even through the door, I can hear my brother grumbling. When they emerge, I take Lang's hand.

My brother rolls his eyes and starts toward the drawing room, leaving us to follow after. "Do you take other forms besides the mouse and the hawk?" I ask Lang.

"Only those two," Lang says. "I wanted most to become a man again. After I achieved that goal, I didn't spend much time learning magics, especially once I realized the cost of the practice. I learned to become a hawk, then I went to become a soldier next."

"But why a hawk?" I ask.

"Because they eat mice," he says. He smiles with his teeth.

"I see," I say as we enter the drawing room. "I think, under the circumstances, I would also want to be a hawk."

He looks at me with one eyebrow crooked. "Would you? It is possible that I could teach you. But you'd have to be prepared for the physical cost. At the very least, you would probably spend a few days unable to lift your arms after the first time you flew."

As soon as he says the words, I want very much to be a hawk. To fly away whenever I like, never again to be trapped and waiting for someone else to come and take me away—I would pay a very high price for that freedom. "I would like that very much," I say.

"Stop your wittering, you two," says Fritz. He pulls back the drapes and cold morning light fills the room, glinting dully on the tinsel and decorations in the Christmas tree. "Look in the cabinet."

We look. On the shelf inside, Mamsell Trudchen sits next to a Columbine doll. Beside them are half a dozen of the toy soldiers Fritz used to play with: the survivors of a full company now leaning against their fellows, the paint of their once-bright uniforms chipped and shabby. Below, the collection of picture books. Above, the dancing dolls Godfather brought to this year's party. The nutcracker, however, is nowhere to be seen in the cabinet.

"Lost your toy, have you, children?"

We all turn. I would swear the drawing room was empty when we entered, but now Godfather Drosselmeier sits in a chair beside the grandfather clock. The great gilded owl seems to spread its wings over his head and shoulders, and the clock's ticking is very loud. It drowns out my heartbeat, or perhaps my heart has stopped momentarily.

Godfather Drosselmeier—here.

But where else did I think he was? I sent him out of the dream world, so of course he must be here in the waking world.

Lang puts his arm around me. My heart beats again. I'm not facing Godfather alone as I did in the orangery of the marzipan castle. This time I have both Lang and Fritz beside me. And last time, even when I was alone, I faced him down and sent him away. Whatever strange magic he has, I'm not going to let him unsettle me now.

"I sent your nephew home to his parents," I say, hoping it is true. "As you should have done long ago, Godfather."

He tilts his head and looks at us. If he were a bird, he wouldn't be a hawk, but a crow: all curiosity and gleaming eye. "Never mind the jumping jack," he says. "Have you my key, Mariechen? I would like it back."

"What key?" I ask, even as my mind is racing to determine where it is. The key he dropped in the orangery when I sent him away. If it's not lost in the snow, it must be with my golden chain in the coat I wrapped around Clärchen, but I'm the only one who knows it.

"My key," Godfather repeats.

"I don't have a key," I say.

He leans back in the chair and studies me with his single eye. I stare back at him. Will he admit to having been in the Kingdom of Dolls? He's always denied his part in the magical world, but maybe now, when Lang and I are both here to confront him, when even practical Fritz believes us, he will acknowledge what he has done. He built the mousetraps that killed Lang's brothers and then he made them part of a bedtime story for me. Did he do it only at the king's request, or for some other reason? Does he regret it?

There is no remorse on Godfather's face as Lang stands before him, though. All these years I believed the mouse king was the monster at my bedside, when it was Godfather Drosselmeier instead. Are there more deaths besides Lang's brothers on his account? More lives beyond his nephew's and mine that he's thrown into disarray? No, I decide, he shall not have his key back, whatever he wants it for.

"Perhaps you dropped it somewhere," I say. "Shall we help you look?"

He doesn't answer, but he shifts his gaze from me to Lang. The tall clock behind him whirs and begins to strike. The wings of the owl move, and Godfather seems to sit up taller, to become somehow larger. When the reverberations of the last bell fade away, he says, "You have the look of your mother."

"I wouldn't know," Lang replies. "I never had the opportunity to see her true face."

"She was a handsome woman," Godfather says. His face softens for the briefest moment, then his gaze turns sharp again. "Have you my key, mouse king?" he asks.

"I do not have your key," Lang says. "I have your curse." His voice is even, but I can feel a nervous twitch of energy where our bodies press together.

Godfather frowns and begins to recite one of his rhymes.
"Bells, ring. Bells, sing—"

Before he can start the second line, however, Lang speaks over him.

"Clockmaker, dream-taker,
Empty heart child-breaker—
Your time is done, your fate is come.
You shall end as I was begun."

As soon as the last word leaves his lips, Lang sags heavily against me, and I struggle to keep him upright. The best I can do is control his fall.

Godfather scowls at us. He leans forward—and forward, and forward. He, too, is falling. His form shifts, and by the time he hits the floor, he is a mangy gray mouse skittering across the carpet towards us.

I scrabble backwards, trying to pull Lang with me. I don't want to touch the mouse. I don't want it to touch me or Lang. Can I kick it, even if it is Godfather?

Maunzi is the one to save me from my dilemma. He darts from beneath the Christmas tree and smacks at the mouse with his paw. The creature squeaks and runs to the side, but Maunzi jumps into its path and swats it again, sending it soaring into the air. When it hits the carpet, the cat pounces, grabs it in his jaws, and shakes it violently.

"Maunzi!" Fritz cries. "Drop it!"

But Maunzi is no obedient hound. He takes his new plaything and gallops out of my brother's reach, back under the spreading branches of the Christmas tree.

"He will eat the head," I say. "He always eats the heads." In the summer, I find tiny headless corpses in the garden.

"Ugh," Fritz says. He looks a little green, and I feel nauseous myself.

From beneath the tree, I hear the unmistakable crunch of small bones and wince. Fritz scrunches up his face. "Ugh," he says again.

At my side, Lang groans and pushes himself back into a seated position. "It is no more than he deserved," he says. His face is pale, and there is a cold sweat on his brow.

"You should get back to bed," I tell him. "Fritz, help me."

My brother comes over, and together we haul Lang back to his feet. "Do you faint every time you do magic?" Fritz asks him.

"I don't usually do so much in such a short period of time," Lang says peevishly.

At this moment, my father pokes his head into the drawing room. "What is going on?" he asks. He looks at Lang, supported between me and Fritz. "Lieutenant Lang, you should be in bed. Herr Wendelstern was quite insistent that you need rest."

"I expect the good doctor is correct," Lang says. He gives my father a rueful smile. "I thought I heard something, and I wanted to be of assistance to my generous hosts."

"The best assistance would be to stay in bed," Fritz says. "Let's get you back there." He gives me a meaningful look, and I step away from Lang to let my brother lift him up instead.

The two of them stagger out of the drawing room, and my father raises an eyebrow at me. "Quite the young hero," he says. "Was he coming to your assistance, Mariechen?"

"I was chasing Maunzi," I say. "He caught a mouse, and I wanted him to take it outside."

My father sighs. "Are we going to have another round of mouse troubles?" he asks. "I'll have to ask your godfather to set up his clockwork traps again."

"It was the first mouse I've seen in the house in a long time," I say. "And Maunzi dispatched it quickly. We don't need traps while we have a cat."

"Very well." My father rubs his temples. "I'll be glad to save your mother the worry. She's upset enough after yesterday's excitement about you and Clara."

Clara—Clara will need me. "Will she go to see Luise and Clara after breakfast?" I ask. "I'll go with her." I can give my niece what I didn't have: an adult who will believe the strange events she has experienced. I excuse myself, and go to dress for the day and all that will need doing.

EPILOGUE

O N New Year's Eve, my family gathers in the drawing room after dinner. The grandfather clock with its great owl on top has stopped working, and since no one but Maunzi knows where Godfather is, it hasn't been fixed. My father brings the mantel-piece clock in from the back parlor and sets it in the middle of the table. Everyone takes their seats around it to watch the final minutes of the old year.

I sit next to Lang. Luise sits across from me and eyes us speculatively.

"I think it's time for auguries," she says. "Let's see what the new year will bring us."

I blush, because I know she suspects Lang is holding my hand under the table. She hasn't said a word to me about Ernst Hatt since Fritz and I brought Lang back to our house.

So much has happened in the last week that to contemplate a whole year's worth of the future seems an impossible task. Still, I nod. "Yes, let's do auguries for the new year."

I let go of Lang's hand and go to the kitchen. I take an old silver spoon from the drawer and fill a bowl with water. When I return, my mother has produced the wooden box with last year's auguries inside and is setting it on the table.

Clara immediately leans forward, trying to see into the box. Johann pulls her back before she can accidentally overturn any of the candles. "Be patient, Clärchen," he says. "You'll see in a moment."

My mother tilts the misshapen lumps of lead out onto the table in front of them. Clara picks up one shiny piece and inspects it. "What's this one?" she asks.

"What do you think it is?" Fritz asks.

She squints. "A flower," she says.

I'm fairly certain it's a piece that we decided was a nail last year, but I don't say anything. If she sees a flower, then a flower it shall be.

"Who will be first?" my mother asks.

"Clärchen," I say, for it's not really a question. I hand her the spoon and resume my seat. "Put the flower on it and we'll see what it turns into this year."

As soon as I'm settled, Lang's fingers find mine beneath the table, and we link ourselves together. He has not returned to the garrison and I have not been so careless as to be discovered sleeping anywhere other than my own bed again, but I want to touch him all the time.

I especially want to hold on to him now, when our time is growing short. Tomorrow is the first day of the new year, and the last day of the soldiers' leave. Lang and Fritz and all the rest of the men who have been here over the holiday will return to their camps and garrisons, to the training and drilling their commanding officers require ahead of the summer campaigns. What will happen after that? It's part of the future that seems so big that I haven't been able to contemplate it. Lang and I have been spending our time in the present moment; we haven't talked about what will happen when the leave is done.

"I'll help you hold the spoon, Clärchen," Johann says. He folds his hand around his daughter's small one, and together they hold the silver spoon over the flame of a candle until the lead softens into a shiny puddle. Then he guides her hand to tip the liquid metal into the bowl of water.

Almost as soon as the lead splashes down, Clara is fishing it out again.

"What is it, Schätzchen?" I ask. "Set it on the table so we can all see."

She puts her lump on the tablecloth, where it makes a damp spot. "It's a pig," she says proudly.

"A pig is very lucky," Lang says, and she beams at him. The influence of the nutcracker's words against him has faded quickly: Lieutenant Lang is a friend of her favorite uncle, Fritz, and now a friend of mine, too, so she's decided he cannot be so bad.

Everyone agrees that the shiny lump is definitely a pig, and that Clara will have a whole year of good luck.

Luise pushes the spoon across the table to me. "Now you, Marie."

What will my future bring? I'm suddenly hesitant to see what the melted lead will augur for the coming year. I squeeze Lang's fingers under the table and pass the spoon to him instead.

"Let Lieutenant Lang try next," I say. "He is a guest, after all."

He smiles at me, then takes up the spoon and one of last year's lumps. Clara is walking her pig across the table, but she looks on with interest to see what shape Lang fishes out of the bowl. His is more flat, with a few long spires lifting up on the sides.

"Trees?" suggests Luise.

My father, though, reaches out and turns it over, so it balances on the spires. "A table," he pronounces. "You will be welcome to sit down with whomever you meet, Lieutenant Lang, as you are welcome to share our table."

Lang inclines his head. "Thank you, Herr Stahlbaum." He hands me the spoon and nudges my knee with his. "Your turn,

Mademoiselle Stahlbaum."

I'm still hesitant to see a portent of the future, but I take up three of the smaller lumps and watch as they lose their individual shapes and join into one circle in the hollow of the spoon. Then I shift the spoon over the bowl and pour the lead into the water.

The shape I retrieve is a near-symmetrical splash. I hold it up for all to see. "A bird," I say, looking at the suggestion of spreading wings.

Luise bites her lip. I know she was hoping I would get a ring, and if I'm honest, I did try to move the spoon in a circle, though I didn't want to be too obvious about it.

"Oh," says my mother. "Mariechen, are you going to fly away from us this year?"

Lang presses my leg again, and I think of his promise to teach me how to become a hawk. I don't care how sore my arms will be—I want to soar through the sky, to see the world from a new angle, to feel the wind around me. "Maybe," I say. Then, because I don't want to worry her, I add, "But I won't fly too far just yet."

I give the spoon to Fritz and take Lang's hand under the table again. He rubs his thumb over my palm in slow circles, and I wish we were alone so I could lean against his solid form.

Fritz gets a boot, which we decide means he will travel. Then Luise's lead comes out as a nest with an egg, and she and Johann and my mother all get misty-eyed at the prospect of another child.

My father claims he is a philosopher and cannot possibly take part in this superstitious ritual, but my mother takes the spoon and announces that she'll try for both of them.

The candle is nearly done. Everyone watches as she lets the lead fall into the bowl. "Who wants to guess?" she asks.

"A chicken to play with my pig," says Clara.

"A door," suggests Luise, "open to new people."

My mother puts her hand into the water and lifts out her shape. It is long and branching. "A tree," I say.

She nods. "Yes, I think so. A tree, full of fruit."

"What about you, Papa?" Clara asks Johann, but he shakes his head.

"I'll share in Mama's fortune," he says. "It's almost midnight, and the candle is going out."

"Time to get your coat on, Schmusebacke," Fritz tells Clara.

Luise and I gather pots and pans from the kitchen while the others dress for the cold outside. Then we go out to the street in front of the house. Our neighbors are spilling out of their houses as well, everyone jolly with food and drink and calling out to one another. Midnight arrives: the church bells begin to ring, and everyone in the city adds to the noise, beating on pots and pans and anything else that will clash and clang.

Fritz and Lang uncoil long leather whips and go into the middle of the street to swing them in wide arcs that end in thunderous cracks. They are drowned out by the booming of the baker beating on a huge dough mixing vat that he's rolled out into the street. Then that sound, too, disappears into the chaos of booms and bangs as people begin lighting off fireworks.

The sky fills with flashes of light, each successive explosion illuminating growing clouds of smoke. Clara clamps her hands over her ears, then runs to Luise, who presses her close. I set my spoon and pot on the front steps and look up at the sparkling lights.

Lang comes to stand with me. Everyone is staring up at the sky, so I lean back against him. He wraps his arms around me, and we look up at the fireworks together.

He puts his mouth close to my ear and asks, "Do you want to fly away?"

With my gaze turned upward, I try to imagine what it might be like to fly above the city and see the fireworks rising from below like bubbles in a boiling pot—only they would be bubbles made of light. I twist in Lang's arms so I can look into his face. Fireworks flash green and white and gold over his features. The colors sparkle in his eyes, reminding me that he is a creature of magic—but he's not a creature. He is a man, and one who is offering me a share of magic for my own.

"Yes," I say. "I want to fly away."

He smiles and leans forward to kiss me. He tastes of burnt sugar and spiced wine, and I want to keep kissing him until the sun comes up late tomorrow, but the fireworks are fading away. The city's arsenal is exhausted, at least until the next holiday.

I pull away, putting a more proper distance between us as my family starts to head indoors again. Still, we two are the last in the door. "In the spring," Lang says to me, "when the snow melts and new things grow, I will return and teach you how to fly."

"In the spring," I say back to him, making it a promise.

He catches one of my hands as I pull off my mittens and presses something into my palm. I look down, though from its shape I already know what it is: one of his seven rings. It glints in the lamplight, and when I slip it onto my finger, it fits perfectly.

ACKNOWLEDGEMENTS

I OWE a great debt to the Seattle Fiction Writers for their continued feedback and encouragement along my writing journey; to Sarah Pesce for her thoughtful edits; and especially to my parents, who took us to see *The Nutcracker* ballet every year when I was small.

AUTHOR'S NOTE

As with so many people, 2020 was a serious disruption to my work flow. I'm extremely lucky that my child was young enough to return to daycare, that no one in our immediate family fell ill, and that I was able to channel my real world anxiety into an escapist fantasy world with Marie, the nutcracker, and the mouse king.

I hadn't seen the ballet since I was a kid, but I let my toddler watch an animated version, because why not? We listened to the music, the kidlet got really into the battle scene, and we watched a lot of YouTube clips together. Suddenly, I was thinking about how creepy Drosselmeier was, and how satisfying it would be if the Mouse King actually turned out to be a hero trying to save Clara from whatever shenanigans Drosselmeier and the nutcracker are obviously up to.

I'll just write a holiday novella, I thought. *Something quick and fun*, I thought, *and then I'll get back to the historical romance I'm supposed to be writing.*

I started researching the original German story and watched a few versions of the ballet. Then I started writing. The "quick holiday novella" quickly ran long and became the first in a trilogy of novels. Everything about 2020 went on longer than expected, after all, but at least this is something fun to share!

A few notes about the story:

First, you should definitely not play with molten lead! Internet research tells me that Germans are encouraged to do their New Year's fortune telling with less toxic wax or tin these days.

Second, as this is a fantasy story, I've mashed together a little German mensur, or academic fencing, and a lot of the more Anglo-Irish-American Code Duello that I assume my readership is more familiar with. It's in *Hamilton*, after all! I assume this will probably annoy some readers, *sorrynotsorry*. I hope we can at least agree that it is an inadvisable way to settle disputes in contemporary times.

Third, the only part of the backstory for Lang and his mother that I made up was the direct blood connection to the human royal family. The original German novella, by E.A. Hoffman, is truly bizarre. I don't speak German, but I consulted multiple translations for this book, which means a few details will make a smidge more sense if you've read Hoffman. In lieu of actually reading Hoffman, however, I recommend listening to Episode 167 of the *Myths and Legends Podcast*, "Cracked," for a 45-minute version that largely coincides with my own interpretation of the story.

Lastly, why are they calling young ladies "mademoiselle" in a nineteenth century German city-state? Short answer: Napoleon. Longer answer: With the caveat that I have played fast and loose with military history, a coalition of German/Bavarian forces joined the French against the Austrian Empire for the War of the Fifth Coalition in the summer of 1809. There's more about that in the next two books, though!

Irene Davis
November 2021

P.S. Can you take a few minutes to review this book in

the usual places online? I love seeing what people think of my books and, more importantly, your reviews help other readers decide on their next book!

CONNECT WITH IRENE

W EBSITE

WWW.IRENEDAVISBOOKS.COM

N EWSLETTER

WWW.IRENEDAVISBOOKS.COM/NEWSLETTER

I NSTAGRAM

WWW.INSTAGRAM.COM/IRENEDAVISBOOKS

HAWK AND HOUND

PREVIEW

CHAPTER ONE

I SIT up in bed, trying to remember what pulled me from sleep back to the waking world.

Was it something in a dream? I've fallen into dreams, and fallen out of them, more than once. This isn't one of those times.

The fire is out, and there's a chill to the air in my bedchamber. The moon lays silvered shadows across the floor, making the shapes of the furnishings uncanny. My chair, my dressing table—the mirror shows something I can't quite identify from this angle.

There's no sound in the night. Just the strange stillness of the small hours when everyone is asleep and none of the usual noises of the city filter through the windows and walls of my family's house.

I pull the bedclothes around me, intending to snuggle down into sleep again. When I wake, there will be the bustle of horses and wagons in the street, the murmur of voices in the house, maybe even an early spring bird singing outside my window.

Before I close my eyes, though, one of the shadows moves. I stare at it, my fingers suddenly cold against the quilted coverlet on the bed. Did I imagine it?

No, for there it is again: a shadowy form sliding over the floor.

It has the shape of a man, but no man should be in my bed-chamber in the middle of the night. Dietrich Lang, maybe—but he's far away in the winter garrison, and he won't skulk in the shadows when he returns. He'll stride through the front door in company with my brother.

The figure approaches my bed, gliding from shadow to shadow without taking a single step. The moonlight doesn't illuminate its face. Maybe it doesn't have one.

I hold myself in absolute stillness, hoping it will dissolve or simply pass me by. I could scream. My parents would come to save me from the terrors of the night, as if I were still a child. But if they come running and this thing has already gone, they'll only add it to the long list of unbelievable stories I've told.

For the first time in many years, I miss the days when I shared a bedchamber with my older sister Luise. Whatever is in my room is ten thousand times worse for my being alone with it.

The shadow-shape is beside my bed now, a blur of deeper darkness beside a pool of cold silver light on the carpet. I hold my breath and try to control a shiver.

"Marie," it says, and I know that voice.

"Godfather Drosselmeier?" I whisper on an uncertain exhale. "But you're dead."

"What of it?" the shadow asks.

"You cannot be here," I say, willing it to be true. He was turned into a mouse, and my cat Maunzi carried him away. I heard the crunch of his bones breaking—and now his ghost is here, in the house where he met his fate.

"Where is my key?" it asks.

The key—the little golden key I picked up from the floor after I banished Godfather Drosselmeier from the Kingdom of Dolls. It was the last thing he was seeking before he died.

"What use is it to you?" I ask. I can't bring myself to say

what I'm really thinking: What use are earthly objects to the dead?

"Give it to me," says the ghost.

I shake my head. "I don't have it." Not with me, anyway. It's in the pocket of my winter coat, a strange talisman of all the adventure that happened at Christmas last year. Sometimes I rub it between my fingers, just to feel the solid metal shape of it and remember the existence of the nutcracker's realm.

"It *is* here," the ghost says insistently. "My key. You must have it."

"I can't give it to you," I say, trying to fill the words with confidence.

The ghost shifts from side to side, as if it might flow forward onto the bed. If I don't give up the key, what will it do? Will it grasp me, or pass through my skin and chill my blood? Even the thought of its undead touch raises goosebumps on my flesh. I try to remember any stories I've heard about ghosts, but nothing comes to mind—I've never liked such tales and rarely stayed to listen to them.

"The Mouse King," it hisses.

"No!" I say quickly. "He doesn't have it."

"Then where?" the ghost asks, its dry voice cracking with anger.

I don't want the ghost to go after Lang, or, worse, to remember that my niece Clara was there in the Kingdom of Dolls too. I have to distract it somehow.

In life, Godfather was always keen to explain how his creations worked and what his tools were for. He told my brother and me the tale of the nutcracker and the mouse king, after all, even his own part in the whole bloody affair. If I can start the ghost on an explanation of what clever clockwork device it made for the key to wind, or what arduous journey it undertook to get the key, then perhaps it will forget its thought about Lang.

"What is the key for?" I ask desperately.

A chill silence is the ghost's only answer. The moment stretches on long enough that I yawn, then blink desperately to clear my vision. Has the ghost gone?

No, it's still there, black and brooding. I don't want it to search out Lang. Or Clara—I can't let anything else frighten her. She suffered enough terror with the nutcracker and the giant Leckermaul. A minute ago, I was wishing as hard as I could that the ghost would disappear. Now I want to keep it here, discover its purpose, and make certain it won't go frightening anyone else in its quest for the key that lies secreted in my coat in the great wardrobe downstairs.

"What is it for?" I ask again.

"Keys are for opening locks and winding springs," the ghost says finally.

That's hardly any information, but at least it made an answer. "Which locks does your key open?" I ask. "Which springs does it wind?"

"It's mine," the ghost says. I recognize the peevishness in its voice, an emotion my brother Fritz and I often inspired in our godfather. Neither of us—Fritz especially—were ever grateful enough for the clockwork toys he brought us to look at. But the ghost can't make clockworks now, nor could it use a key to wind toys or open locks.

Neither has it come any closer to me since it first spoke. Why doesn't it just float over and make a further threat? Something holds it back, and the idea makes me bold.

Slowly, I release my tight grip on the bedclothes and sit back more comfortably. "And what would you do with your key if you had it back, Godfather?" I ask.

The ghost sways again, menacing me but still not actually approaching.

"My key," it says, but there is a note of uncertainty in its voice.

"You don't know, do you?" I say. "You are nothing but an

echo."

"Give it to me," the ghost says again.

"No," I say. "You haven't answered my questions."

The more it presses, the more curious I become. Suppose the key does have a use beyond winding Godfather's clockworks? What would he have done with it if he hadn't met his untimely end as the cat's plaything? Nothing good, I expect. I could get out of bed, fetch the key, and hand it over to the ghost, but I don't think I will. Godfather lost the key in the dream world, meddling where he shouldn't have been, and I found it. It's mine now, and I won't give it up to the wandering echo of a grim old man.

The tale of Godfather Drosselmeier's life has ended, but mine hasn't. I intend to have plenty more adventures, and perhaps I'll find a way to make use of the key. I haven't gone back to his workshop since that terrible cold day in midwinter, but maybe I should go and look. What other magic might I discover?

There is a small creak from my bedchamber door. I know the sound well: it means Maunzi has pushed it with his head, opening it just wide enough for the cat to slip through.

"Tell me about the key, Godfather," I say. There must be a story behind the key, if I can only find the way to trigger its telling from the ghost. "Is it magic?"

The ghost moves agitatedly. "My key," it says. "My key."

Then Maunzi leaps up on the bed, and the ghost shrieks. The high, unearthly sound pierces through the night stillness. The cat pins his ears back and returns a full-throated feline battle cry. The ghost shrieks again as Maunzi leaps at its shadowy form—and then it's gone.

The cat lands on the empty carpet in the pool of moonlight. He growls, but there's nothing for him to battle against. Instead, his tail lashes the air angrily as he looks about the darkened room.

I sit frozen in bed for long minutes, peering into the shadows and waiting for the shade to return. When it doesn't, I climb out of bed and stroke Maunzi's back.

His spine is stiff, and his fur stands out like a chimney brush. He meows, sounding more mournful than bloodthirsty now. I coax him back to the bed and sit with him on my lap.

Both of us continue staring into the night. I smooth the cat's fur and think about the key, remembering its shape and feel in my hand.

The key is no bigger than my little finger. Whatever it opens must be small. Maybe it does nothing more than wind one of Godfather's clockwork creations. But which clockwork, and what would make it so important that his ghost would return to seek it? I still can't decide if the ghost is truly Godfather Drosselmeier, or merely an echo of his last thoughts. Either way, it has managed to convince me that the key is far more valuable than I'd guessed.

The patches of moonlight slide across the floor. Maunzi gradually relaxes into sleep. I let my fingers rest in his warm fur.

I wish Lang were here. If anyone I know would have an idea what to do about a ghost or a magical key, it would be him.

Lang promised he would return to me in the spring, and the snow is nearly gone. He and Fritz and the rest of the soldiers must come soon. They will have a last leave before the next campaign begins. Lang will come and teach me to fly, and if the ghost returns, we will face it down together, as we rescued Clara from the Kingdom of Dolls together.

Despite my unsettled thoughts, I fall asleep again sometime before dawn. When I wake, my mother stands over me.

"I don't know how you can sleep so late," she says, tugging the coverlet away from me and shaking her head. "Breakfast was over ages ago! Time to rise and dress. I'll not have a daughter of mine spending her days in bed."

I blink at her and rub my face. Maunzi is gone, and spring

sunshine is spilling from the blue sky into the room. My body is stiff from sleeping sitting up, and my neck is sore. I consider asking my mother if she heard anything peculiar in the night—surely Maunzi's furious yowl must have woken someone else in the house—but I discard the idea immediately.

If I try to tell her I was visited by a ghost, she'll only shake her head and tell me to put it out of my mind. My parents have always believed that my strange adventures are only fantastic and childish dreams. I can't convince them of the truth of my experiences. Instead, I stay silent in hopes that I can at least convince them that I am a woman grown and not a child.

"Yes, Mother," I say and get out of bed.

CHAPTER TWO

AFTER my mother leaves, I dress and hurry downstairs. No one is in the front vestibule, so I open the wardrobe and feel about until I can slip my hand into the pocket of my coat. My fingers close around cool metal.

Quickly, I unclasp the golden chain I wear about my neck and thread the key on it so that it rests next to the ring Lang gave me. Then, I tuck them both beneath my bodice and head to the kitchen. Even if breakfast has been cleared away from the dining room, I know Dora will have saved me some food.

After I've eaten, I go out into the city. At first, I begin automatically walking toward the Wendelsterns' home, where I'll find my best friend Trudy. Before I'm halfway, though, I stop and move to the side of the street.

I've told Trudy the story of my first and second adventures in the Kingdom of Dolls, but I haven't told anyone about the golden key. There's a part of me that wants to have a secret just because it's a secret, not because no one would believe it. The key is real. I could hand it to Trudy and let her hold it, but I find I want to keep it for myself a bit longer. Besides, if I go to Godfather's workshop first, perhaps I will have more of a story to tell her.

I turn and head up a different street, then stop again. Clara. What if the ghost went from my bedchamber to the nursery where my niece lay sleeping? I should run to my sister's house. No, I should run home, find Maunzi, and take the cat to Luise's.

But how will I explain to my sister that I want her to keep the cat locked in the nursery? Or to Clara herself? I don't want Clärchen to think there is anything to worry about.

And aside from scolding me for sleeping late, my mother was in good humor this morning. Luise would have sent a message to our house if there was any trouble. And I know she keeps a close eye on her daughter after the terrifying day Clara spent in the Kingdom of Dolls.

I take a deep breath and smooth my hands over the blue wool of my coat, feeling the way the fabric has warmed in the bright sunshine. I am the one who has the key. If the ghost comes for anyone, it will come for me. Or for Lang, if it remembers the grudge it holds against Lang's family.

The key—I want to take it out and examine it, except now it is hanging around my neck, closer and yet less accessible than when it was in my coat pocket. What does the key wind? It seems too small to unlock any door or padlock. More likely it goes to one of the clockworks that Godfather left behind, but which one?

If there's an answer, it will be in the workshop. I start walking again.

I wish I could tell myself that the ghost's visit last night was nothing more than a dream. I've tried to blend my life back into the everyday cares of my family and friends and not think too much about the magic I know exists in the world—but I've kept the golden key in my pocket and Lang's ring close to my heart since the end of our adventures at Christmastime. Now, it's time to see if I can learn a few of the secrets my godfather left behind.

I try not to look into the shadows as I pass through the

city. The sky above me is bright. The meltwater from the last of the snow shines molten silver-white in the sun. New plants are pushing up, bright and green against last year's dead remnants. Lambs and chicks are preparing to come into the world.

I'm ready for Lang to return. He hasn't written to me, but I have his ring. I can still hear his promise to teach me to fly.

Again, I look up into the sky where the spring sun is burning away a few wisps of puffy cloud. What would it be like to take to the wing and slide through the air with the spring wind? I close my eyes for a moment, calling up the memory of Lang slicing through the sky and harrying the giant away from the nutcracker's ruined castle tower. That will be me. I will fly and swoop and go out into the world.

When I open my eyes, Godfather Drosselmeier's workshop is before me, the building held close between its neighbors. The wooden sign, carved with the face of a clock, moves slightly in the breeze. This is where he lived and worked, repairing clocks and making the mechanical toys that both fascinated and disturbed me in my childhood. This is where the nutcracker fled after his disastrous duel with Lang, and where Clara was taken into the Kingdom of Dolls.

Other houses have everything open to let the spring air in and the staleness of winter out, but the windows of the workshop are shuttered, and the door is closed. I try to imagine what it will be inside: dark and chill, musty after being closed up for so many months. It will be full of shadows—and what will the shadows be filled with?

Maunzi frightened the ghost out of my bedchamber, but where would it have gone, except to crouch and rustle here, in the darkness of its own domain?

I hesitate in the street, looking at the remnant crust of ice on the front step. There is no sign of footprints on the slick surface. No one else has dared to come here and disturb whatever is inside the workshop. What clues will Godfather have left behind?

I step up, and the ice cracks to wet shards beneath my boots. With my heart pounding in my ears, I press the latch—and it doesn't open.

I stand in the slush and look at the iron lock. My heart is pounding, the blood rushing loudly in my ears. At Christmastime, nothing stopped me and Fritz from entering to look for Godfather Drosselmeier, his nephew, and little Clara. Did Godfather lock the door one last time before he came to our house to ask me and Lang about his key? Did someone else close it up after he failed to return home?

I'm not sure if I feel more relieved or disappointed that I don't know where the rest of Godfather's keys are. He must have had others. The little golden key is far too small to even bother trying on the door. Anyone passing by would laugh at me—or demand to know where I'd gotten the key from. I want to learn more about the key, but the lingering memory of the ghost's midnight visit makes me shiver despite the warm spring sun.

What if the ghost has more power in the workshop than it had in my room? What if I step into the darkness and it knows somehow that I have the key with me? I imagine the icy touch of a dead hand reaching through my clothing to grasp the key where it lies next to my heart, and shiver.

The crunch of footsteps breaks the hold of my imagination. It's our neighbor Theda Doerffer, walking towards the square with her market basket on her arm and her sharp eyes on me. As soon as I look in her direction, she detours toward me.

"Has Herr Drosselmeier returned?" she asks.

It's been three months since anyone saw my godfather in our city, and before last night I never expected to see him again. I don't know exactly what the ghost is, nor do I know what the extent of its powers are. In any case, though, I'm not about to discuss it with Frau Doerffer. "It doesn't look like he has," I say.

"Perhaps he went back to Nuremberg," she suggests. "I've heard that's where he came from. He had relatives there, didn't he?"

"Did he?" I echo back to her. I don't want to give her anything more to gossip about than she'll already have after seeing me here.

Still, her question sends my thoughts to young Drosselmeier, my godfather's nephew. He was from Nuremberg too, but is he there now? I have no idea what happened to him after he flung himself into battle with the giant Leckermaul in the Kingdom of Dolls.

Instead of answering, I point to Frau Doerffer's basket. "Do you think there will be spring onions at the market? Or strawberries?"

"It's much too early for strawberries," she tells me, and that, for now, is enough to divert her attention. I walk with her to the market square, listening to her advice about the earliest berries and where to find them.

Godfather's workshop can wait until Fritz and Lang come. I'm sure that Fritz will be able to figure out who has the keys to open it, and Lang will know something of how to deal with a ghost.

It takes half an hour to end the conversation with Frau Doerffer and return home. I come through the stables, hoping to find my brother's stallion, Fox, but there is only our gelding Brandt, and Flora the nanny goat with her swollen belly. I scratch Brandt beneath his mane and give Flora an extra portion of hay, then go into the house.

As I'm taking off my coat in the vestibule, though, my father comes in and raises an eyebrow at me.

"Isn't it Wednesday?" he asks. "Is your sewing circle canceled?"

I stop unbuttoning my coat. Is it Wednesday? The encounter with the ghost unsettled me so much that I couldn't think of anything else when I woke. "No, Father," I say. "I went out for a walk this morning and came back to get my sewing bag."

It's only a small lie. I can't tell my father I was visited by the ghost of his old friend anymore than I can explain that Godfather Drosselmeier was eaten by the cat. I've heard my parents discussing; with his absence stretching out, some of Godfather's creditors have come to my father looking for news of him. Like Frau Doerffer, my father thinks he went back to Nuremberg for some reason of his own. I could tell him differently, of course, but no one has asked me. What could I possibly know?

"Father," I call after him before he goes down the hall to his study, "has Luise sent any word today? Is she well?"

He looks at me, still smiling at my forgetfulness. "Your sister is well," he says. "Your mother went to visit her this morning. I'm sure she'll tell you all the feminine details when you return."

CHAPTER THREE

I FETCH my sewing bag and leave again, hurrying through the streets to the Aschenbrandts' home. Petra and Magda welcome me; Trudy is already seated in the parlor with her two younger sisters and a few other young women.

"Will Luise come today?" Petra asks.

I shake my head. "I don't think so." My sister is expecting her second child, but the pregnancy has not been an easy one so far. She's made few social calls lately.

Magda makes a sympathetic noise. "I hope she feels better soon," she says. "On the other hand, perhaps the rest of us will accomplish more when we aren't comparing our poor work to hers."

"I'll tell her you speak so kindly of her," I promise. Luise makes beautiful things, and she gives each a single-minded focus that I can't match. I can make small, straight stitches, but only until my mind wanders to some other topic than the cloth in my hand. I find myself unpicking nearly as many stitches as I put in.

I go over to Trudy, who is laying out colors for something new, shades of pink and yellow arranged on her lap. As I sit down and open my own sewing bag, she holds up two of the yellows.

"Are these the right color for primroses, do you think?" she asks.

I point to the lighter skein. "That one."

Trudy nods. "That's what I was thinking."

She sets the floss down again. I take out the muslin fichu I have been working on. The whitework is nearly finished; I've already made curling vines and flowers around the whole thing. What remains is finishing the edges, which I've decided I want to be scalloped, and adding eyelets. The triangle of delicate fabric spreads across my lap like wings. I thread my needle and pick up one side.

The other girls have their places around the parlor, sitting on the sofas and chairs. Only Petra is without a sewing project. Her place is at the writing desk near the window, where she has fresh pens and a stack of precious paper.

"Who has a story today?" Petra asks, uncapping her inkwell. She looks around the room. I feel her gaze linger on me, and my throat goes dry. I have a story, if I want to share it. I have many stories, but I don't tell my own tales at the sewing circle. Perhaps I should. I could change a few things here and there, tell my adventures as if they occurred to a princess or a poor peasant girl who was whisked away to a magical kingdom.

Before I can convince myself to speak up, Trudy's middle sister Mathilde does. "I have a story," she says, and begins. "There was once a poor man and his wife who lived at the edge of the forest."

That's how all the stories start.

There was once a king and a queen who had no children…
There was once a girl who was lost in the forest…
There was once a young man who went out into the world…

Sometimes I catch a detail here or there and recognize that the girl telling the story is spinning something from her own experience, but none of us tell these kinds of stories about ourselves. It's always "There was once…" and never "*I* once…"

It's easier that way. If it's not about yourself, then it doesn't matter so much if no one believes it, if someone laughs at an event that made you sad or sighs at something that lifted your own heart.

I bend my head and listen to Mathilde tell her story, keeping my fingers busy with my sewing. As long as I'm listening, my needle moves easily. It's only when there's nothing else to distract my mind that it wanders away to my own fantastic experiences and I forget to tug my stitches tight.

Mathilde is halfway through her story, with little children collecting white pebbles in the perpetual dark night of the forest, when Magda looks out the window and interrupts her. "The hussars are here!"

I jerk my thread in surprise and it snaps, but I don't care. The hussars—Lang will be here soon. I'll be able to tell him about the ghost and share the mystery of the golden key. Perhaps he will recognize it—or perhaps we will simply fly away on an adventure, and I will come back to deal with ghosts and finish my needlework some other day.

I fold the half-finished fichu and join the others at the window. In the street below are the green-and-gold uniforms we've been longing for these past three months. Someone elbows me. We all want to get closer to the window, to see their faces and find the ones we've been particularly pining for.

Ernst Hatt, the judge's son, looks up and waves to us. My brother Fritz is beside him on his chestnut stallion, but where is Lang? I scan the faces of the other cavalrymen. Only one man rides a bay horse, but it's not the bald-faced stallion that carried me and Clara and Lang out of the snow in the winter.

Lang must have passed already. I didn't get to the window quickly enough, or Magda didn't notice the first members of the regiment in the street. He'll go to the garrison—or will he come with Fritz to our house?

"Did you see Lieutenant Lang?" Trudy asks me.

"No," I say. "He must have been at the front."

She nods. Her eyes are bright with excitement. Everyone is twittering and sighing. Mathilde's tale of unfortunate children will go unfinished, for no one wants to sit inside sewing now.

"I need to go home," I say, and the others echo my sentiment. The silk threads and muslins are wrapped up and put away hurriedly. Trudy's youngest sister, Anneliese, pricks herself and stands in the center of the room with her finger in her mouth while the rest of us swirl around her. Everyone is talking, but the words don't penetrate into my thoughts.

The soldiers have returned home. How long will they stay before they have to go back to their regiments? Will they come again when the summer ends, or will this be their last leave?

I put on my coat, not bothering to button it, and take my sewing bag. "Goodbye, Petra. Goodbye, Magda. Thank you for the tea."

I hurry home and fly through the gate to our yard. There is my brother, swinging down from Fox's back to stand in the damp brown dregs of last year's grass.

"Welcome home," I say. I hug him. He smells of sweat and horse and damp leather. "Was it hard travel?"

"The roads are miserable," he says. "Rivers of mud. And if you ride through the fields, the farmers set their dogs on you." There are lines beneath his eyes, and his tall boots are muddy. A few spatters of mud even mar his cheeks, though they're not immediately obvious against the day's growth of beard.

We walk through the yard to the stable and he unsaddles his horse. I want to ask him about Dietrich Lang or tell him about Godfather's ghost, but I bite my tongue and help him with Fox instead. Fritz looks too tired to deal with my supernatural problems.

By the time we've cleaned the mud from the stallion's deep brown hide and settled him with fresh hay and a warm blanket against the still-cool spring air, I've almost convinced myself that Lang is at the garrison, that he's giving our family time to greet Fritz before he visits me.

Fritz takes a last look around Fox's stall, then picks up his saddlebags. He slings them over one shoulder, and we leave the horses. At the stable door, he stops and takes my hand. "Mariechen," he says, and there's something in his voice that sends a shiver down my spine.

"What is it?" I ask, even though I don't want to hear what he's about to say.

"Lang isn't coming."

"Why not?" The words come out quickly, before I can pretend that I'm not disappointed.

My brother looks at me. I can feel him measuring his words against the effect he thinks they'll have on my heart. "He has distinguished himself delivering messages exceptionally quickly," Fritz says finally.

"Aren't messengers allowed leave?" I ask.

"Not when the general has taken particular note of him," Fritz says. "General Carville keeps Lang close at hand. If he's not careful, he'll find himself attached to a marshal, and then we'll never catch sight of him again."

"Will he—" I can't finish the question, for I know what the answer must be. If Lang can't be let at liberty now, when the armies haven't yet begun their marches, then there will be no chance to see him until the snows come and the soldiers regroup and resupply during the winter months. And if he falls during one of the summer's battles—but I can't consider that possibility.

Fritz shakes his head. "I'm sorry, Mariechen," he says, squeezing my fingers. He starts to pull me in, as if to hug me again, then stops when I stiffen. "I'm sorry," he repeats.

"Did he send anything for me?" I ask. "A letter?" Surely Lang will have sent me some sign. I should have something from him, something more than the ring. Has he forgotten me so quickly? He can't—Lang holds onto his past so tightly. He forgets nothing. He won't have forgotten me, or the promise he made, and yet he isn't here.

"I'm sorry," my brother says for the third time. He waits, but when I don't say anything, he pats my shoulder and goes into the house.

I stay in the yard. An hour ago, I saw the new growth. Now, everywhere I look, I see only dead grass and leaves left wet and flattened by the weight of the winter's snow.

Want the rest of the story? HAWK AND HOUND is available in ebook and print.

Made in United States
Orlando, FL
13 October 2024

52611796R00125